Jan Mark worked for some time as a secondary-school teacher before starting to write full-time. Her first published book was called *Thunder and Lightnings*. One of her novels, *Eclipse of the Century*, was shortlisted for the Guardian Children's Fiction Award 2000. When she is not writing, Jan spends much of her time in schools and colleges, giving talks about writing, and running workshops with teachers, students and children. She lives in Oxford.

RIDING

JAN MARK

TYCHO

MACMILLAN CHILDREN'S BOOKS

First published 2005 by Macmillan Children's Books

This edition published 2006 by Macmillan Children's Books
a division of Macmillan Publishers Limited
20 New Wharf Road, London N1 9RR
Basingstoke and Oxford
www.panmacmillan.com

Associated companies throughout the world

ISBN-13: 978-0-330-40087-9
ISBN-10: 0-330-40087-8

1 3 5 7 9 8 6 4 2

A CIP catalogue record for this book is available from
the British Library.

Typeset by Intype Libra Ltd
Printed and bound in Great Britain by Mackays of Chatham plc, Kent

For Rebecca

Part One

1

The mainland was so far below the horizon there was no way of knowing that it existed at all. It was 40 kilometres away, people said, but it might have been a hundred kilometres, a million. Still, the mail-boats and freighters must come to the High Island from somewhere, and return there. Those occasional passengers who arrived on the mail-boats, under guard, must also have come from somewhere, although they never went back. Otherwise the mainland could have been a myth, like other stories of strange creatures and distant worlds.

The Low Island, though, was no myth. They could see it all the time, like a ship moored hull down, with just its spars and riding lights showing above the sky-line. By day the watchtowers stood dark against the sunrise and caught the last rays of the sunset, when they seemed to blaze like hot wires. In between, depending on the weather, the structures merged with the clouds or appeared fleetingly as if they had risen out of the sea. On clear nights the lights clustered like hovering stars; when the overcast was low, a sullen glow hung above the island.

They always knew when an escape had been attempted. The hours of their days were measured by hooters, whistles, bells, sounding across the strait. The High Islanders relied on them as much as they did on their own clocks, for timekeeping. Escapes took place at night. The Low Island would explode with light, the Banshee set up its swooping howl over the waters, and at that signal their own lighthouse would be instantly extinguished. Sooner or later there would be shots. Only when the Banshee fell silent could the lighthouse keepers rekindle their lantern.

From where she lay in bed, Demetria could see the upraised finger of the lighthouse, bisecting her window, a column of starlessness. On escape nights, lying awake while the Banshee whooped, she would press her thumbs into her ears and watch for the light to swing into life again. She did not want to hear the shots. Only once, in her eleven years, had the Banshee wailed all night and the lighthouse remained dark until dawn. Nothing had been said. Nothing was ever said, but everybody understood that on that occasion the fleeing man had drowned or got away. No one would ever know for certain, one way or the other. It was safer not to know.

The keepers of the light came from the mainland,

4

men who did not resent the order to douse the one lamp that showed after curfew, the beacon that might give hope to a desperate man alone and fighting for his life in the black sea among the striving currents and undertows. Whether the prisoners chose to live out their lives on the Low Island or end it in the strait, they were all killers and saboteurs. Did they tell themselves that they were escaping or did they know that they were going to their deaths?

On the High Island there were no prisoners, only Politicals, sent out of harm's way to a rock where all communications had been cut, except for written letters delivered in strongboxes.

Demetria could not remember exactly when the Politicals had started to arrive. The prison island and the Banshee, the shots in the dark, were part of her earliest memories because they were the answers to her earliest questions. But another early memory was of a disused packing shed down by the harbour. Between one week's end and the next the place had undergone repairs, the crumbling split-stone roof replaced with sheet metal, a wall built round it with an iron gate. Then the soldiers had moved in and, soon afterwards, the first of the silent, pallid men had been escorted off the mail-boat, which in those days carried letters and parcels in loosely strapped canvas sacks.

He had been billeted with the lighthouse keeper, but not long after that the lighthouse keeper and his family had left the island, to be replaced by the two mainlanders. Anjelica, the lighthouse-keeper's daughter, had been Demetria's particular friend, and for weeks afterwards – it seemed a long while at the time – Demetria had expected a letter. Neither of them could write very well then, but whenever the mail-boat put in she had waited confidently for a message from Anjelica, who never would have gone away without telling her why.

About the time of her seventh birthday, Demetria had been so sure that Anjelica would remember her that she had gone down to the dock to see the boat unloaded, and that was when she discovered that things had changed. That instead of being slung ashore in their easy-going sacks, the letters were sealed in steel boxes, given into the charge of one of the soldiers from the barracks that had been a wool-packing shed.

Had that been the moment when she knew that she would never hear from Anjelica again? Also on that boat had been another of those dazed silent men, this one sent to live at the schoolhouse. Gradually, all over the town, people found their empty rooms and out-buildings requisitioned, and their families increased by one. There was a small payment in return for having a Political in the household since the family was responsible for his food and laundry. You got a bonus, apparently, if you *offered* to take one, with all the extra inconvenience, but Demetria's mother had never offered, and they had never had their own Political – until last week.

The soldiers did not have to wait for mail – they must have some other way of keeping in touch with the mainland – for the day before the mail-boat was due, one of them, a sergeant, had come up the winding street from the quayside and handed Mam a printed letter informing her that she was required to provide lodging and board for a guest. The Political had been brought to them the next day, by which time the shed at the end of the garden had been cleared out by Mam and Demetria, a bed hauled across from the house, a table set up, and a chair. In the corner were a basin on a tripod and a slop bucket.

'Where will he keep his things?' Demetria had asked.

'He will have no things,' Mam said, as if she knew, but she told Bevis to fix hooks behind the door. Even a Political would want to hang up his clothes.

They were at school when the guest arrived. From the kitchen Demetria could see the shed, the louvred window in the stone wall, but her own room faced another way, towards the lighthouse. For six days the guest was unseen; it was still dark when they left for school and growing dark again when they returned. Mam said nothing about him and Demetria knew better than to ask.

She noticed that there was an extra handful of meal in the morning porridge pot, but there was no fourth fish in the pan at supper. The Political was given his dinner at noon, whatever it was. When he chose to eat it was his own affair.

On the seventh day of the the week there was a market down on the quayside and the school was closed. Mam left early on market days to get her goods laid out. The sun was still below the sea when she shook Demetria awake.

'You'll have to take him his breakfast.'

The guest had no name yet.

Demetria did not argue with her mother; even Bevis, three years older, was only just beginning to. But Demetria argued now.

'Can't he have it early?'

Mam was already going downstairs. 'When you hear the work bell from the Low Island, take it across. Not before. There's nowhere to leave it and it's raining. You don't stop to talk, just hand in the tray and come away.'

The street door closed behind her. Demetria looked out at the lighthouse in the blue dusk of daybreak. She could tell by the glow against its flanks that although heavy rain was falling over the High Island, there would be a sunrise out at sea. It happened so often; their peak trapped the clouds and they slopped about in drizzle or a driving downpour, while all around the sunlight skipped and sparkled on wave crests. The only consolation was the promise of a rainbow over the mountain.

8

She went down the stairs to the kitchen and looked along the wet garden to the shed, its stones beginning to gleam in the rising light. On the table stood the breakfast bowls and mugs and a wooden tray to carry out to the guest. The porridge pot was on the stove, steaming, a bubble rising to the surface now and again. The coffee can, with enough in it to keep them going all day, stood beside it. All she had to do was turn a ladle full of porridge into the bowl and pour the coffee – did the guest put milk in his? Some people did. Mam could have told her that much at least.

She could go and ask him.

She did not want to ask him, did not want to speak to him at all nor even to see him. Why must she wait for the bell across the strait? If she put the bowl and mug outside the shed and balanced the tray over them that would keep the rain out long enough for her to rap on the door and run back to the safety of the house before he opened it.

Better still, why couldn't Bevis go? Ah, but he was a man; men needed their sleep. She did not understand why Bevis needed more sleep than she did, or Mam, but it was one of the things that everyone knew.

She dressed, ladled out her own porridge and the guest's, poured her coffee and his, opened the kitchen door and paused on the step, carrying the tray. What she hoped to hear was the morning work bell from the Low Island, but there was only the sound of the

9

rain on roofs, in gutters and puddles. She put her head down, held the tray before her and scurried along the path to the shed. There was no light behind the louvres; still, her knock would wake him. She put the mug and the bowl on the flagstone before the door, propped the tray across to make a roof, knocked sharply and fled back to the house.

As she slammed the kitchen door behind her she realized that when he opened the door of the shed the tray would fall inwards and might upset the mug. Fearfully she went to the window and looked out. It was lighter now, she could see the shed quite plainly, and the tray leaning against the door. The door remained shut.

Hadn't he heard her knock? He was a man, and therefore needed his sleep, but he must be a hungry man. The feeding arrangements told her that much. Wouldn't he have been waiting for that knock? Then she heard footsteps passing in the street. The high garden gate opened and one of the soldiers came in. Demetria shrank against the wall. Was he coming to the house?

The soldier was fumbling with keys. He went down the path to the shed, to the shed door, and finding the tray in the way he kicked it aside before bending to put the key in the lock. He had not seen the crockery under the tray, until it went rolling across the step, but instead of picking it up he turned the key and booted the door open. Then he stood to one side, with his weapon drawn. From the darkness of the doorway stepped the guest, tousled, shambling, the way men were in the early morning. He stood outside, bareheaded in the rain, while the soldier went in. He must have a torch of some kind – she saw the beam sweep around the interior as if he were searching it. Then he came out again, without looking at the guest, walked back up the path and through the gate. As it closed behind him the sun rose and a second or two later she heard the bell ringing across the strait from the Low Island.

The man stood in the doorway looking at the ground, slowly taking in what had happened to his breakfast. He stooped and gathered up the empty bowl, running his finger round the inside of it before putting it on the tray. The porridge was splashed across the stones at his feet and the rain was already washing it away. He reached for the mug which had broken, and laid the pieces regretfully beside the bowl; then he went back into his shed and closed the door.

Demetria peeled herself away from the window, already trembling with fear. Now she knew why she ought to have waited till the bell rang. There were two guilts on her conscience. The guest had no food and she had a broken mug to account for. The one she had filled for herself, she saw now, had been meant for him. It was made of metal.

Why did he not come to the door and ask for more

food? Perhaps it was forbidden, but who would know? Who would tell? Perhaps he thought that she would, if he knew she existed. Had he watched her through the louvres, her craven dash through the rain? Had he known what the soldier would do when he came to unlock the door and search the room before the guest could be allowed out after his cold and lonely night in the dark?

Oh, and what did *she* know now?

2

Her own mug and bowl were waiting on the table. How could she sit by the stove and eat, and drink hot coffee, knowing that their guest had probably had nothing since yesterday noon? He had no fire.

But he need not stay in the shed now. The soldier had not locked him in, so he was, presumably, free to walk out of his door, out of the garden, down into town where he could buy food.

But he would have no money probably. Some Politicals did. They were the ones who lived in houses, who were sometimes seen in the shops down by the harbour. Her shame was growing. Their guest had lived for a week at the end of the garden, and beyond the fact that she knew he was there she had scarcely thought of him. If she and Mam and Bevis had ever had anything to say to each other they might have talked about him while they ate, while Mam knitted, while Demetria darned stockings, but until now he had just been something kept in the shed.

There was enough porridge for one left in the pot, and Bevis knew to the millimetre how far up the bowl his portion came. She had no choice really. Taking up her own bowl and the tin mug she went out again into the garden. The rain was easing, the rainbow fading, but the path was slippery. She walked with great care for if she dropped or slopped this lot there would be no more.

Before she was level with the gate into the street, the door of the shed opened and the man came out, carrying his bucket. When he saw her he held up a warning hand and called angrily, 'Wait there.'

Was he still annoyed about his breakfast? Surely he could see that she was bringing him more. He carried the bucket to the far side of the garden, where the ground fell away steeply, and upended it over the wall. She knew he was angry for himself, not with her, because she had seen him emptying his night soil, so she halted, staring at the wet stones of the path, and did not raise her eyes until she heard him speak again. 'All right. Come on.'

He was in the doorway, holding out the tray so that she could put down the bowl and mug. Then they stood looking at each other. *You don't stop to talk*, Mam had said, but how could she turn away?

She said, 'I didn't know the soldier came to let you out.'

14

'And at sunset, to lock me in again.' His accent was strange, like a mainlander's but different, and his voice was stiff. It creaked, as if opening his mouth was as difficult as opening a door kept closed all winter, swollen with disuse.

'I didn't know.'

'Did you know about the water?'

'Instead of coffee?'

'To wash in. I am allowed to wash.'

'Where is it?'

'I rather thought you'd know that.' He did not smile, that unyielding door again, but she could tell he was being pleasant. 'The lady of the house brings a kettle with the breakfast.'

Mam had not told her that, had forgotten perhaps, had not cared enough to remember. The lady of the house; *Mam*? She looked back along the path, seeing all that he could see of her home, the whitewashed wall which, being on the seaward side, was blank up to the gable except for a small window by the kitchen door. Their own cottage was built against a larger, higher one. He must think it was all one building, a sizeable household, instead of four rooms, two of them in the roof.

'I'll fetch it now.'

It was cold in the garden, but the sun's warmth, wintry and thin though it was, moved the air. A stagnant chill breathed out of the shed. How he must have been longing for hot water – more, perhaps, than for the food. She ran back to the house and took the kettle from the hob. It was heavy, she had to carry it in both hands, spout forwards to avoid a scalding stream if she should slip. There was still no sign of her brother.

The Political was back in the doorway of the shed with his basin, but when he saw that she could not lift the kettle any higher he set it down so that she could pour the water.

'Don't you have a man in the house to do the carrying?'

He sounded as though he knew perfectly well that there was a man in the house, but what was he thinking of?

'Men don't do housework,' she said. Still he did not smile, but she felt that inside he was laughing, and not with amusement. 'You could always come and fetch it.'

'Well, no, I can't. Not yet. Perhaps in time I shall get permission.'

'To come to the kitchen?'

'I'm not really supposed even to be talking to you.' He took the basin inside, set it on the tripod and brought out the empty bowl and mug. In the time it had taken her to fetch the kettle he had eaten his breakfast, the mug drained, the bowl scraped clean.

'I'm sorry about the other mug. Will you get into trouble?'

She shrugged. The details were none of his business. 'Is there anything else I ought to do?' she asked.

'No thank you,' he said gravely. 'Everything's perfect.' He handed her the tray with the spoon, the two bowls, the whole mug and the broken one arranged on it. 'Can you manage the kettle one-handed? No, it's still got water in. We've already broken so many rules one more won't make matters worse.'

He followed her up the path to the kitchen door, carrying the kettle, but he stopped short of the step and handed it through the doorway.

She put it back on the hob, but when she turned he was still standing there.

'You can't come in here but you can go out of the garden?'

'I can go where I like until sunset, so long as I show up here at noon. Anyway, there's nowhere to go.'

'Nowhere?'

'Not for me. Think about it. I'm told things will change. But I really must go back –' he might have been talking about a long journey – 'you never know who's watching.'

'Why shouldn't we talk?'

'It's called fraternizing. It isn't encouraged.' He raised his hand, half wave, half salute, and started to walk away. Then he turned.

'You might just tell me your name.'

'Why?'

'It would be nice to think I knew at least one person here.'

She was not sure that she wanted to tell him. He didn't know her. She gave him a name that nobody used any more.

'Dede.'

'Diddy?'

'De-de. What's yours?'

'*My* name? I don't have one of those at present. I'm 37250. You could call me Three, for short, or Five-O.'

Simultaneously there came a footfall overhead and a drumming at the street door. Bevis! Visitors!

The guest, Three, or Five-O, saw her start and raised his eyebrows. 'I won't tell if you won't.'

She knew that this was not as cosy as it sounded, but there was no time to answer. He was walking back along the path, Bevis was coming down from the loft and whoever was at the street door was knocking again.

'See who it is.' Bevis made straight for the porridge pot. Demetria had the kitchen door shut before he looked up, and ran to open the other. It might be a neighbour, but a neighbour would knock once and go away again if no one came. It might be a soldier – but a soldier need not even knock, although most of them tried to be civil.

She dragged the door open and found Devlin on the step, one of Bevis's friends from school.

'Is your brother awake yet?' He winked at her. Suddenly things were ordinary again.

'He's just got up.'

'Lazy beast. Oi! Bevis!' he called over her shoulder. 'There's a log fall coming in, should be with us in an hour. Are you fit to come down?'

Bevis called back something from the kitchen.

'I suppose that was yes,' Devlin said. He raised his voice again. 'I'll see you down at the Point then – in time for the next hooter.'

The hooter sounded on the hour from the Low Island.

'Can I come too?' Demetria said. She wanted a good reason to be away from the house. Anyone could go down to the beach, but if she went uninvited Bevis might decide to send her back.

'We can't have a little thing like you hauling logs,' Devlin said gallantly. 'Your arms would be out of their sockets and how would you knit then?'

Demetria thought of the kettle she had lugged down the path.

'I'm strong in the shoulders. Anyway, it won't just be logs, will it?'

He laughed at her. 'Were you expecting something then?'

'Of course not.'

'Well, no one can stop you if your mam doesn't mind. See you later. See you later, Bev!' he called,

19

over her head, and bounded down the steps, down the street.

Would Mam mind? Demetria hadn't been told to stay at home; once the chores were done she was as entitled to her day off as anyone else. But had things changed because of the guest? Ought she to leave the house empty? But he would never know that the house was empty and he seemed to understand the rules; or at least, understand when he was breaking them.

She remembered his parting words: *I won't tell if you won't.* Who could he tell? She had disobeyed Mam; who was he disobeying?

Bevis sat at the table, unhurriedly spooning porridge into his face, and did not look up as she went to the sink to scour out the porridge pot. Through the window she saw the shed, the closed door, the louvred window. They were on the edge of spring, when days would lengthen, grow warmer. But how would the guest keep warm when winter came again and the wind tore in through the unglazed louvres? Would he still be with them when next winter came? How long did guests stay? So far as she knew, none of them had gone away again although she had heard that one of them might have drowned.

'Who were you talking to?' Bevis said, behind her. She jumped.

'When?'

'When I came down you were talking to someone in the garden.'

Her mind began to twirl. *I won't tell if you won't.*

'I suppose it was the Political. Didn't Mam say you weren't to speak to him?'

'I wasn't really speaking—'

'And why was he down at this end of the garden?'

'It was the kettle . . . too heavy . . .'

'Did Mam tell you to take him a kettle?'

'No, he asked – I think she forgot.'

'If she didn't tell you to fetch him a kettle you shouldn't have fetched it. We don't take orders from his sort.'

'It wasn't an order.'

'They aren't allowed to ask for things either.'

'How can I know that? Nobody explains.'

'You don't need explanations, you just do as you're told,' Bevis said. His eyes had strayed to the tray by the sink. '*You* do the explaining. Who broke the mug, you or him?'

'I did.' It had been the soldier, but it was her fault.

'Liar. I'd have heard it.'

'In the garden.'

'You shouldn't have taken it into the garden. Why do you think he has the tin mug and bowl and a wooden spoon, eh? So he can't cut himself, that's why.'

'Why should he cut himself?'

21

'Work it out,' Bevis said. 'Those hooks we put in the door, they had to come out again.'

'He couldn't be cut on them.'

'But he could hang himself,' Bevis said. 'They're supposed to stay alive.'

She cleaned out the pot, the dishes and the mugs, still without looking round, so that Bevis would have finished his breakfast and left without her knowing, except that he paused and gave her a clout across the back of her neck.

'That's for the mug, in case you forget to tell Mam.' His hand came back the other way. 'And that's for anything I don't know about.'

Demetria still refused to look round. She was watching the shed, the window, the door, and seeing – although she could not see him – a man so desperate that he would want to die. How could anyone *want* to die?

She banked up the stove, swept the floor, washed the windows and scrubbed the table, and was at the short clothes line, outside the kitchen door, hanging out the cloths, when the hooter from the Low Island sounded across the strait. Devlin had thought the logs would be in by now.

Their hillside street was so steep that it was built in long steps, so that the shepherds' pack animals, laden with fleeces, would not slip. She left the garden by the side gate and ran down it, skipping from step to step. At the second corner, between two houses, she could see down to the Point at the end of the beach. And there were the logs, like a shoal of great sea creatures, just coming into sight as though they had navigated their way across the ocean from wherever it was they came, to make landfall at the one place on the island where they could beach themselves, or at least be welcomed and conducted to shore, or harpooned if they didn't come quietly. They would not be alone. The current that brought the logs, to be stored and dried ready for next winter, delivered other things, as though it knew what the islanders needed. Calm summer waters brought few gifts, but towards autumn came seaweed in great stinking heaps, in time to be spread on the fields and dug into gardens for compost, and all year round there were unexpected treasures cast up on the shore. Sometimes there was a corpse rolling in the surf, to be taken away for hasty burial.

Leaving the road, Demetria took the short cut to the beach between the low stone walls of gardens and small fields. From the high, steep path she could see men in dinghies, out among the logs, and boys like Bevis and Devlin, ready on the shoreline with grappling hooks and ropes; others were making their way from the town to gather in the harvest.

She hurried to join them, wondering, as she often did, where the logs came from. There was no point in asking anyone, she knew what the answer would be: 'Tycho brings them.'

3

The best logs were captured by the men in dinghies who rowed out to intercept them with harpoons and ropes and chains. As soon as a log was speared it would be towed to shore. The big ones were taken by men working in pairs, to be shared out, or by the occasional lone hero skilful enough to manage both his boat and the monster single-handed. The smaller ones were left to reach the shallows, where people would wade out, and in warmer weather, swim out to claim them.

With the logs came bark, great curling sheets of it, shards, slabs, some loosely connected by nets and strings of fibre. No one went out to fetch in the bark, it floated ashore of its own accord, where women and children could gather it up. Such luck that this latest log fall should arrive on a seventh day when there were so many people around to harvest it. The market would have emptied as everyone hurried to the beach; even schoolchildren were free to join in. It was a real tragedy when there were not enough men to go out after the giants, but the fishing boats were all in dock today.

Even now, Demetria saw, there was one log that was going to get away. It had come round at an odd angle, a long way from the rest of the shoal. If no one got to it soon, and most boats were already bringing their captives to land, it would cruise on past the beach, past the mole and the harbour, and on round into the strait to be lost forever. No one would dare to pursue it because any boat that sailed between the isles was likely to be fired on. If the log ever touched land again it would be on the far side of the High Island, on the rocks at the foot of the vertical cliffs. Not even a log the size of that one would be worth the risk of climbing down the sheer rock face, and what could they do with it even if they caught it?

There were tales of cliff descents, attempts to rescue shipwreck survivors, that always ended badly. Stories never had happy endings. No one would go down after a log.

Mam was not among the women splashing in the shallows to drag in the bark. As a fisherman's widow she was entitled to a share of anyone's haul. A length of each log was kept back for the community stack down by the harbour. The Town Fathers delivered it for the asking, nobody grudged it, but Mam hated to ask. She always sent Bevis or Demetria when their stock ran low. Bevis too hated asking. That was why he and Devlin were out there now, up to their thighs in the icy water, wrestling with a fat slippery dolphin. The smaller logs were called dolphins, the big ones whales. Demetria did not know why. Divided between them the log would provide enough wood to save them asking for a handout for weeks. Devlin too had lost his father.

Demetria had brought a sack. Without stopping to greet anyone she ran the last few metres across the shingly sand and began grubbing up bark. The Coveneys from down the street had raised a cairn of it between the five of them, as tall as the eldest, Brodie, who was now organizing the others to carry it away. The biggest pieces had gone already but there was plenty left; it all had to be split up anyway. Demetria was quite happy with the smaller bits and the sack filled quickly. Even waterlogged, the bark was still fairly light.

If she took it home now there would be time to come back for another load. She dared not leave it while she collected more. People liked to think that there was an unspoken agreement among the bark-gatherers that no one should touch a pile collected by anyone else, but she did not trust the Coveneys.

She tied the neck of the sack, swung it over her shoulder and set off up the beach towards the path. As soon as she began to climb she discovered that the sack was heavier than she had thought; one lump of bark had a sharp corner that dug into her shoulder and then, when she shifted it, into her neck. She would *not* give in and drag it behind her as a small child would. Head down she stumped on upwards, breathing hard, and did not see that there was someone standing in the way until she reached the place where she had paused earlier to look down on the beach, where the field walls began.

'May I carry that for you?'

Gasping for breath she stopped short in surprise and let go of the sack. It bounced as it hit the ground and immediately began to roll on the steep path. The person who had spoken sprang past her, overtook it and stopped it with his foot, although he slipped and almost fell as he did so. He had not expected the muddy grass to be so greasy.

It was the guest.

What was he talking about, as if carrying the sack would be a favour to her?

'No,' she said. 'We do it ourselves.'

'You mean no one is allowed to help – or *I'm* not allowed to help?'

The sack was between them. He was now lower down on the path than she was. Their eyes were level.

'I don't know. Aren't you?'

'Probably not.' He looked more cheerful, well, healthier, than he had done when she saw him last, but it was hard to tell what he was really like under

27

the scrub of his beard. Why wear a beard when you didn't have to, and all rough and straggly like that? But if he wasn't allowed sharp objects he wouldn't be able to shave. Bevis wouldn't pity him. He was always rubbing his thumb across his chin, hoping for bristles.

'Are you allowed out here?' she said.

'So long as I'm back at noon, when the guard comes to check. That's why the food arrives then, to lure me back. And he comes to tuck me up at sunset.'

'Tuck you up?'

'After a fashion.'

It must be nearly noon. Mam had not said anything about the guest's dinner. Either she intended to be home to see to it or he was meant to go without. She picked up the sack again, turned and began the next stage of the climb.

'Well, may I walk back with you?'

She did not say yes or no. She could not stop him walking behind her, but he need not think he was wanted.

'What was all that about?'

'What?' He must know that she was out of breath, but so was he, and he wasn't carrying anything.

'The logs. Does it happen often?'

'No.'

'How often?'

'Sometimes.'

'Do you know when they're coming?'

28

'Yes.'

'How?'

'Someone sees them.'

'They're not regular then?'

'Regular?'

The path turned here and widened. They were not many metres from the street. He came alongside.

'You don't know to the day when they'll come?'

'Of course not.'

The slope was levelling out. 'Tycho brings them,' she added.

'Who's Tycho?'

'The drift.'

'The *what*? Oh, the current. There's a current called Tycho?'

Didn't he know *anything*? 'Tycho and Kepler, those are our drifts. Kepler brings the fish. Tycho brings the logs.'

'Well, all things considered, I'd call that very handsome of Tycho. What would you do for wood otherwise? This is about the tallest tree I've seen.' They were passing the thorn that twisted over the path where it met the roadway. 'Or are there bigger ones inland?'

'I don't know.'

'I suppose the wind keeps them short and bent sideways like that.'

'Does it?' She had never thought about it, but his suggestion made sense. When winter set in, the wind was often so strong that even the shortest people went about bowed down by it. Why wouldn't a tree, out of doors in all weathers, do the same?

'So, what did you do for fuel before the logs started coming?'

How he did go on. 'They've always come.'

'Do you know, Dede, I don't think they have,' the guest said, but she did not answer. They were walking up the street now, the house was just coming into view, and Mam was standing in the doorway. The gate to the garden was open too. A soldier was standing there.

'Is he waiting for you? Will you be punished?'

'Yes, he's waiting for me. No, I won't be punished. So long as I'm back when the hooter—'

Over on the prison island the throaty voice of the hooter barked once – twice – a third time. The guest quickened his pace and went on ahead to meet his guard, leaving Demetria to face Mam alone.

'What were you doing with him?'

'I wasn't with him.'

The first slap landed. 'You were with him.'

It was no use to protest but she had to explain. 'I went down to the beach for bark. I met him on the way back – he was on the path – watching. He has to be back by noon, that's why—'

The second slap cut her off.

'Who broke the mug?'

'I did.'

Third slap. 'That's for the mug. Put the bark away and go to your dinner.'

The bark was kept in the log store beside the earth closet. Demetria emptied the sack and hung it to dry on the line. The soldier was just leaving. As she went into the kitchen Mam came out carrying the guest's dinner: bread and cheese and a bit of smoked fish, another mug of coffee. That was all he would get until tomorrow morning unless he went down into the town and . . . was *that* what he was meant to do, beg? Was that what happened to the guests who had no money? Were they given the choice to beg or go hungry? No one went begging. It was the first thing you were taught, pretty near: earn or go without; never ask for help. That was why Mam so hated asking for wood even though she was entitled to it; why they always had less than they needed, unless they could get their own.

When Mam came back Demetria said, 'Bevis and Devlin have got a dolphin.'

'I should hope so,' Mam said. 'From what I hear it's a good shoal.'

Demetria's face was still burning from the slaps, but if she kept talking perhaps everything would be all right again. 'There's mountains of bark. Shall I go back and get some more?'

'Eat your dinner.'

'I could take it with me. And Bevis's too. Him and Devlin . . . the log . . .'

31

'Eat it. Then you can go back. If these mountains are so high there'll be plenty left.'

Not if the Coveneys had anything to do with it; they could organize themselves in relays. Didn't Mam *want* her to get more bark? Of course she did, but even more she wanted Demetria to do as she was told. She knew she had been punished for walking with the guest, but Mam didn't know yet that she had talked to him as well, this morning. With luck the punishment would cover her in advance if Bevis blabbed.

When the meal was finished she washed up.

'Can I go now?'

'Aren't you taking the sack?'

She fetched it and went out again. She had nearly given herself away. Yes, she would gather bark, but the beach would be emptier now, as the logs were hauled into town to be sawn and divided. Now was the time to see what else Tycho had brought, for in the wake of the logs came other things. Logs were logs, but there was no telling what else might arrive to be examined, kept, traded, sold. Some of the things were so strange they were unidentifiable, some half destroyed, but all desirable because, like the logs, they were a gift from the sea, delivered by Tycho, that brought them what they needed most, but took so much in return. At the very least she might find something to give back to it at the death of the old year.

There were few people on the beach now, the indefatigable Coveneys and one or two other children whose parents were lax about dinner times. They came from homes where there was more food on the table, where missing a meal did not mean going hungry.

Demetria wandered along the water's edge. The beach was little more than seven or eight hundred metres long, a shallow crescent where Tycho had scraped out the one place on the island where you could walk out into the water. At one end it was enclosed by the Point, rocks that had fallen from the cliffs, and at the other were more rocks that cut it off from the harbour where the mole reached a crooked arm into the sea. On the far side of the quay were yet more rocks, where the Blackwater ran down into the harbour, and then cliffs again, all the way round in a sheer unclimbable wall. In a way, Tycho's bay was its other gift to them, besides the logs. Without it there would be no way on or off the island, no place to have built a harbour.

Very little had come in with the logs this time, apart from the usual scattering of slake horns, the spiral tusks, no longer than a baby's finger, of the little fish that played in the shallows. She found the remains of a woven basket, a flat wooden box with the top gone, bottles, bones. Nothing to keep and treasure, hide if necessary, as she had once kept and treasured oddly shaped bits of wood and coloured stones.

Still, one of the bottles was pretty, with patterns in

the glass. If nothing else, she could give it to Mam for an offering when the year died, in a couple of weeks. It was dying in good time this year, on the sixth day, which would make two days running off school. That in itself was rare enough to be wonderful.

4

The rocks beyond the harbour had come down from higher up the mountainside, time out of mind, as if emptied from a gigantic sack, like potatoes, still lying where they had fallen. Waves and wind had worn them into smooth curves on the seaward side, but some still had flat surfaces and sharp edges, twice a man's height, and there was one great level slab like a paving stone, only it was five metres across. To one side of it was a hollow, roughly the shape of a person lying at full stretch, roughly the shape of a grave, and once every 300 days that was what it became – the grave of the old year.

On the last day of the year the whole town went down to the grave and placed some object in it, for themselves or on behalf of the family. There was no ceremony unless a family chose to make it one for their own reasons, but unless you went down at first light you became part of a long line that wound from the harbour steps, around and over the rocks, to the grave. Early comers could take any route they pleased, but once the queue had formed it became an orderly procession.

Demetria would have liked to go down early, to be there on the rocks as the sun rose, perhaps alone, the very first at the grave, but Mam insisted that all household work was to be done before the three of them set out down the hill, washed, brushed and wearing their best clothes. There were only two cottages further up and Mam would never leave the house until those families had gone past. People were apt to be chatty on Old Year's Day; they would try to draw her into conversations. Mam did not believe in conversations unless there was something to say, and when she had said it she stopped talking.

By then it would be mid-morning, the busiest time. Waiting in line meant talking too. They could not see the harbour or the rocks from the house, so from time to time Demetria would be sent down to the second corner to see if the queue were long or short, and at last, when there was no chance of getting involved with anyone else, they would set out. Demetria's greatest fear was that one day they would leave it too late and, unthinkably, they would fail to get there before sunset. If you did that there was no point in going at all; the moment was past, you had missed your chance. There might be no logs for you in the coming year, a landslip might take your home or your life. It was the fisher families who had the most to lose. They would never risk being too late with their old-year offering, were usually the first to make it down to the rocks; but it did not always work. Four weeks before Demetria had been born her father and the rest of his crew had been lost on the far side of the island, taken by Kepler and never seen again.

Demetria was looking forward to Old Year's Day and not only because of the extra long holiday this year. There was always a general air of relaxation, almost of festivity, and sometimes nice food. Mam never did anything special, but Demetria enjoyed hearing people at school discussing their own small plans.

After the events of log-fall day she was happy to be back in the routine of school, rising in the dark, going down to the town as the sun came up, back again in the red light of its setting, hearing the hooter from the Low Island and feeling secure in the knowledge that before she got home the soldier would have made his evening visit and the guest was once again something they kept in the shed, none of her business, not her responsibility. Last market day she had followed Mam's instructions to the letter, waiting for the soldier to arrive and depart before leaving the food and running back to the house. When 37250 opened his door she was safely in the kitchen. Bevis fetched the tray in later. No one did anything about the kettle.

*

When the day came to bury the old year, Mam sent Demetria down to the corner to check on the queue just as the first hooter was sounding. This made her think of the guest; how would 37250 be spending the holiday? Since the Politicals had begun to arrive they sometimes came down to watch and one or two were known to have made offerings themselves. What did they expect from that? Demetria wondered. They were not islanders, the sea would not care what they did. They owed it nothing; whatever it sent was not for them.

She glanced at the shed as she went out of the gate, but 37250 did not emerge or follow her down to the corner where she could look out over roofs and walls to the harbour and the rocks where the year's grave lay.

The dark rope of people coiling over the rocks was well short of the quayside, but when Demetria got back to the house Mam was still sweeping the stairs and Bevis was enjoying a leisurely wash at the sink. There was no question of leaving for another hour at the earliest. On the way down to the corner for the second time Demetria saw a soldier coming up towards her. All the soldiers talked funny, they were not islanders, but this one had to repeat his question twice before she understood what he was asking.

'Are you the Joyce girl? Is your guest at home?'

She had no idea. The soldier himself was more likely to know than she was.

'I think so.' Why was the soldier coming to see him now, it was nowhere near noon? On this of all days she would not mistake the time.

He smiled at her – they all smiled at children, it seemed to be part of their orders – and went on up the street, his boots pounding out every step. Demetria stopped and watched him turn in at the gate in the garden wall before hurrying down to the corner again.

The queue had lengthened a little and by the time they got down there a couple of families like the Coveneys might have strung it out further, but she could tell Mam truthfully that there had not been many people there when she looked. But best to hurry. She started back up the hill as the soldier started down, keeping her head lowered so that she would not have to see him if he smiled this time. But she was curious. It was still not noon, so why had he been up to the house – no – to the shed? He was not taking the guest away with him.

When she reached home she found out. Bursting in at the front door she saw Mam at the kitchen door, talking to the guest. Demetria did not need to see the set of Mam's shoulders to know that she did not want to be talking to him. He must have come down from the shed and knocked at the door.

'How did you get the letter?' she was saying. 'There's no mail-boat today.'

'I don't know when it came,' he said. 'These things

take time to be processed. They just told me to pass it on to you.'

Demetria saw that there was a letter lying on the kitchen table, half opened out.

He went on, 'And they've sent money. I can pay you more now. Laundry . . .'

Mam was answering very low, as if trying not to speak at all. Demetria edged towards the table. She could just see the beginning of the letter, covered in official-looking stamps at the top of the paper.

Madam, to inform you that 37250 Ianto Morgan has been reassigned Category B status pending . . .

He had a name. Something had happened, something that had brought him and his name to the door. She longed to tweak the paper a little and find out more, but one eye was on Mam and the doorway. The guest, Ianto Morgan, was moving away. Mam was going to close the door.

Demetria stepped back a pace or two. Mam would have heard her come in, there was no point in pretending that she had just arrived, but she could at least distance herself from the letter. Then she saw Bevis on the stairs, watching her for something he could hold over her if she stepped out of line.

Mam turned from the door. Bevis came down the last few steps.

'He's been reclassified,' Mam said over Demetria's

head. 'No privileges, but they've released his money and he has to report to the barracks twice a day.'

'He'll be paying you extra then,' Bevis said, also over Demetria's head.

'He will, but he needn't expect more than food and laundry for it. I'm not having him in the house; it isn't expected.'

'At least we won't have the shark up here all hours.' The soldiers were known as sharks, out of their hearing, although they must know about it. It was an odd word, it had a somehow savage sound, but the soldiers did not seem to be savage. 'Why did he come to the door? Did he think you'd ask him in?'

'To give me that –' Mam nodded towards the letter on the table – 'and to introduce himself, if you please. As if I cared.'

Bevis looked at the letter, unfolding it. As the man of the house he had a right to see anything that came into it.

'Ianto Morgan; is that what we call him?'

'We don't call him anything,' Mam said. 'We don't want to encourage him.' She seemed to see Demetria for the first time. 'Nothing's changed,' she said. 'You stay away from him.'

'Who?' If she was not supposed to know then she would not know.

Mam looked at her coldly. All right then, she did know.

'The line's quite short now,' she said. 'Can we go down?'

They did not discuss 37250 Ianto Morgan on the way to the harbour. The midday hooter sounded before they came out on to the quay where the boats lay at their moorings like piglets alongside a sow. They all had eyes painted on either side of the prow so that they seemed to be squinting down their bowsprits at anyone who looked at them. No boat put out on Old Year's Day unless it were for a rescue, but who would need rescuing on the last day? Everyone was here.

'I thought you said the line was short.'

'It was when I saw it.'

They ought to have set out at once; more people had arrived before them.

'When will you learn to stop lying?' Bevis said lazily. Demetria knew better than to protest. Bevis knew that she had not lied, but if there were an argument she was the one who would get her head smacked.

Bevis was carrying the decorative bottle that Tycho had brought. It had no value, offerings did not need to be valuable; it was the thought that counted. Some people, though, people with a special secret hope, might put something treasured in the grave, but it would be something treasured only by them, not worth money.

They joined the line. Mam returned the greeting of

the woman in front and then talked to Bevis in case the woman wanted to continue chatting. As they had nothing to talk about it was a stilted conversation, a word jerked out now and again as they moved forward over the rocks. Mam was knitting, all the women were, needles flickering, the balls of yarn twitching like trapped fish in the work bags that they wore tied round their waists like aprons. Standing idly in the queue there was no excuse not to knit, and it gave families a chance to compare notes. Every man would expect his wife to be the fastest knitter there, and all the women were openly eyeing each other's hands. The girls were knitting, too, but no one was looking at their work, although some of the older ones were as fast as their mothers. Demetria was not one of those.

If people had just dropped things into the grave as they went by, the line would have moved faster, but it was considered polite to wait at the edge of the flat slab until the person ahead of you had gone to the grave and walked back again. When it was their turn, Mam followed Bevis and Demetria followed Mam. They were not abreast until they reached the graveside.

It was almost full. By the end of the day people would not be dropping things in but placing them carefully on the low mound of gifts that would have risen in the grave. Demetria looked down at the stew of shoes, gloves, small coins, toys, bits of crockery, a

43

knife. Whatever you gave might be old but it had to be whole. There was a beautiful white shell, crimped and curled; Demetria longed to handle it and quashed the longing instantly. What was in the grave had been given to the sea; the sea already owned it, even if it might be some time before it came and collected its gifts. Take anything out and perhaps the sea would one day come to claim it back. Bevis stooped and dropped the bottle so that it landed on a glove and not on something that might break.

Afterwards there was no need to stay together. Bevis met up with Devlin and some other friends on the quayside. Most people stood around in groups, talking; men with men and women with women, but Mam would never stop to join them. She was already on her way across the quayside, still knitting furiously, to go back up the hill without looking round to see if Demetria had followed. A short way off some Politicals, in pairs, had come to watch the grave fill up, from a respectful distance. It was forbidden for more than two to be together. Some of them must have been here last year and were explaining to the newcomers what was going on. Their own Political, 37250 Ianto Morgan, was not among them. Why should he be? He probably did not know that today was special; who would have told him?

Demetria did not follow her mother. Some of the girls from school had started the hop-toad game on the quayside. Usually the place was so busy there was no room to lay out the course without getting in the way, and they could play hop-toad only in the cramped yard round the school. This was the one day of the year when they could go where they liked and already the course meandered all over the flagstones. It was simple enough to play, you could play it alone, but the more people joined in the more competitive it became. All you needed was a flat pebble and a piece of white softstone. The first girl drew a circle round where she stood and tossed the pebble as far as she thought she could jump. If she were right and reached it, she drew another circle and threw again, and again, leaving a trail of circles, until she overestimated herself and the pebble went to the next girl, who had to follow her from circle to circle as far as she could. People with short legs, who knew their limitations, did not throw far, but the taller ones left long spaces between the circles. If you couldn't leap the gap you dropped out until your turn came again. Meanwhile the trail of circles grew longer, weaving from side to side, looping and backtracking.

Demetria tacked herself on to the line behind Devlin's sister, Stephane, who sat beside her in school. The smaller girls had given up now and were jumping about alongside the line, yelling encouragement to their favourite toads. Some of the boys were sitting on the school wall, jeering impartially but most loudly at the big girls, as if they could not bear to see their sisters enjoying themselves at something which was of no use to boys. The girls could not knit while they played. They all had their knitting bags slung round their waists, of course, but the knitting was safely buttoned inside. Demetria, like the others, slid hers round so that it hung behind, out of the way while she jumped. The boys seemed to resent that more than anything. 'Who's got a tail?' they were shouting.

She did quite well on her first hop, better on the second. She knew she had no chance of completing the whole course and throwing the pebble herself, she ought to have started sooner, but it was worth trying and glorious when she brought off a difficult leap and the little ones cheered her. If only there was some work for women that involved rushing about. Herdswomen did, she supposed, but there was no likelihood of being allowed up into the highlands to look for a job. Anyway, rushing about would be more fun if they weren't so swaddled and padded, buckled and buttoned into winter clothes: frocks, trousers, sweaters, scarves, coats. The only time they could go without those was in the few hot weeks of summer, and that was almost half a year away.

'I've had enough,' Stephane said when Demetria came back to join her the third time.

'We've only just started.'

'*You* have. I've been here for *hours*. You stay if you like, I'm going to get a bun.'

'I'll come with you – I've got some money.' Even Mam did not grudge a few coins to spend on Old

46

Year's Day or, if she did grudge them, she still handed them over.

As they walked to the bakery Demetria noticed that some of the Politicals, two by two, were now watching the hop-toads, and some mothers, also noticing, were calling their daughters away; some brothers, too, jumping at the chance to flex their muscles. One girl refused to stop. It was Audrey, the tallest and lithest, the one who threw the pebble furthest because she knew she could reach it from a standing start. Her brother first called her out of the game, then came over when she ignored him, pushed through the small girls and grabbed her plait. She was just landing and, jerked off balance, fell awkwardly, skinning her palm. Her brother hauled her to her feet, but instead of following him meekly she did a crazy thing and raised her arm as if to hit him. The blow did not land, but he turned and hit her, backhanded across the face, and she fell again.

No one protested; it happened all the time. It was Audrey's own fault for not obeying her brother even though he was younger, but one of the Politicals started forward. Immediately his friend pulled him back, but already the other brothers were surging across the quayside, scattering the hop-toads and gathering in a threatening group, balling their fists, flexing their knees. Even Bevis was among them, although no one had besmirched Demetria's honour and he would not have cared if they had.

Audrey, crying, was already huddling with her friend Josephine, moving quickly out of the way; the little girls were scrambling for safety, but there were running footsteps coming the other way and across the stones ran a detachment of soldiers, weapons raised, between the little group of bewildered Politicals and the brothers who were pumping their elbows, bouncing up and down on the balls of their feet, stoking their rage.

Stephane tugged at Demetria's arm.

'Come on, there might be shooting. Come *away*.'

She scuttled towards the bakery, dragging Demetria behind her. Demetria kept looking round. There would be no shooting. The Politicals did not want a fight and hadn't meant to start one. The boys knew better than to argue with armed men. One of the top soldiers, with sergeant's chevrons on his sleeve, was ordering the Politicals to disperse – not just to leave but to separate from each other. The boys saw that and swaggered bow-legged as they strutted away in a bunch, as if they had had their fight and won it.

5

The quayside was almost deserted now. A few stragglers were still making their way to the grave, but most of the grown-ups had gone home; the big girls had retreated, the little ones had fled to their mothers. The boys were still prowling about as if patrolling conquered territory, but their imagined enemies, the Politicals, were nowhere to be seen.

Demetria and Stephane took their buns and sat on the harbour wall, feet dangling over the thick greenish water where it shouldered and shifted between the boats. Stephane kept looking behind her nervously.

'What's the matter? No one's going to push us in.' It had been Demetria's idea to sit here; she did not want Stephane complaining about it.

'They might.'

'Not into the sea, not today.' The boys only liked to hurt, they would not try to kill, and no one took liberties with the sea, especially where girls were concerned. Everyone knew that if women fell into the water they sank like anchors. Only men could float.

They ate the buns very slowly. These were just the same buns that they got on any other day, that their mothers made, but these had been paid for with their own money; that made them special.

Since Anjelica the lighthouse-keeper's daughter had vanished so suddenly, Stephane had become Demetria's best friend. This was partly because they shared a desk at school and partly because Devlin didn't mind. Some boys could be very fussy about the company their sisters kept; fortunately not even Bevis could object to Stephane. And Stephane was never cruel when they played the looking-glass game. There was rumoured to be a glass in the barber's shop, but only men went there. Girls were not encouraged to look at themselves. No one had a mirror at home.

The looking-glass game was played in pairs. Stephane wanted to play it now. 'Tell me how I look.'

Demetria stared back. You had to start off with the ordinary things. 'Your hair's yellow.' All islanders were blond, that was easy. 'Your eyes are blue and they go up at the corners. You've got a brown spot under your left eye. Your nose comes to a point – open your mouth. That side tooth's gone, but it only shows when you smile. The new one's coming through.'

'What about the chipped one?'

'It's still chipped. That sore place under your chin's nearly healed.'

'Good. Your turn.'

Demetria hesitated. Stephane was not cruel but she was honest. Still, once you had agreed to play you had to take your turn. Some girls got you to play so they could say something hateful. 'Tell me how I look.'

'Your eyes are round and your eyebrows go right up like someone made you jump. Your nose is flat. Your mouth is wide like a hop-toad.'

Not too bad. It was always the same after Mam had done her hair. Demetria was sure that her eyes would not look so startled, her nose so flat, her mouth so wide, if her hair were not plaited so tightly, stretching the skin of her face. They all wore their hair in long single plaits, but Stephane's was loosely woven and soft. After Mam had washed Demetria's hair she braided it tightly into twenty-seven little torturous twists that became nine, then three, drawn to the top of her head and then into one long heavy rope that hung down between her shoulders. There it would stay for four weeks, but just as the twenty-seven twists were growing out, slack and comfortable, it would all be unravelled, washed and bound up again, still wet.

She sometimes felt it must be a punishment for sins she had not yet committed. Mam had done it fresh last night, ready for Old Year's Day, yanking, tugging, twisting in angry silence. Demetria's wide eyes still watered at the memory. No one else had such an elaborate arrangement, and no one else, she was sure, suffered so much for it, but Stephane never said it looked nice.

'. . . and your black eye's nearly faded.'

Demetria had not known that she had a black eye. It must have been one of the slaps she got after talking to the guest – two weeks ago. No wonder it was fading. There was still a bit of bun left. Should she eat it in one satisfying mouthful or make it last in a series of tasteless nibbles?

'What will you do tomorrow?' Stephane said.

'I don't know.' They contemplated the next day in silence, the luxury of two consecutive holidays.

'It won't be the same next year.'

'It might.'

'I don't remember it ever happening before. Old Year's Day might be on a Senday next year, and we'll only get the one holiday.'

'I don't think that's allowed,' Demetria said.

'But how do they know when it's Old Year's Day anyway?'

'It's the shortest, isn't it?'

'Is it? How can they tell then?'

'It must be the hooter,' Demetria said. 'They must know the shortest time between the work bell and the sunset hooter, so when we get to the *next* shortest time, then tomorrow's Old Year's Day.'

'But . . .' Stephane was struggling with an idea. 'How did they know . . . before the island . . . ?'

'It's always been there.'

'I mean the prison. I know the island's always been there, like ours, but there wasn't always a prison on it.'

'Wasn't there?'

'Someone must have built it. It didn't just grow.'

Of course someone had built it, but Demetria had always assumed vaguely that prisoners had moved into it and it had become a prison, the way the packing shed had become a barracks when the soldiers arrived. She did not want the conversation to go any further. It was the kind of thing they got into trouble for at school, asking questions to which there were no answers, or questions to which they were not supposed to know the answers, as when they tried to find out about carpentry and seamanship – things the boys did. 'You don't need to know that,' they would be told. School was not the place for asking questions. Come to think of it, nowhere was. If there was no answer it was stupid to ask the question. What was the point of asking about navigation when girls could not understand such things. And the Low Island was a place no one ever asked questions about. Demetria herded the last crumbs together in the palm of her hand and picked them off one by one with the tip of her tongue.

Stephane had already finished her bun. 'Do you want to come to the beach? Tycho might have brought us something.'

'We could play hop-toad here, now. On our own.'

'No . . .' Stephane glanced over her shoulder again. There were still a few boys loafing against the wall, kicking stones, and Devlin was no longer there to look out for them. 'No, I'm going to the beach. It'll be dark soon.'

'I'll see you tomorrow, I expect.'

Stephane stood up and walked away. That was the trouble with the longed-for holidays. There was nothing that you *had* to do, but nothing much else to do, either, even with a best friend. Demetria looked the nearest boat in the eye. How did it feel to be out on the sea in one of those narrow rocking sheds, under a swelling sail, riding the Kepler drift to follow the fish, gliding home again on Tycho? She would never know; women did not go on the water because they could not swim and there was no question of hiding in the bottom of a boat, under nets, in a barrel or a coil of rope. No boat ever put out from the harbour until it had been searched from stem to stern by soldiers working in pairs. Two more stood guard at the end of the mole, where they had a little hut, to make sure that no one tried to get on board later.

She heard the fishermen talking about their vessels, how each had its own strong will and strange habits; how one would swim wherever you sent it and another buck and strain to go its own way. They looked the same to her, except for the names, painted just behind the eyes: *Polty, Burl, Great Orn, Sarling, Slake*. They were all named after fish.

She could walk out along the mole to watch the sun sink into the sea again, which at this time of year was not so very far from where it had risen this morning. But as the chill day turned to cold evening the wind was getting up, the water was beginning to be agitated out beyond the harbour mouth. Even the boats were starting to jostle at their moorings. Round by the rocks there could be waves; if she stayed long enough, not till dark but until the sun was down, she might watch the sea take its first gifts from the grave.

It was a long while since the last person had made an offering, so she would have the place to herself. She swung her feet round and stood up. Even the boys had wandered away now and the soldiers were back in their barracks. Demetria crossed the quayside and started to climb the rocks, the way they had come this morning. Long before she reached the grave she could see it, on the far side of the flat slab, no longer a hollow but a multicoloured mound and beyond it, in the low light, a sudden dash of spray as the first hoped-for wave struck against the stone lip of the island. At times of calm the grave might lie undisturbed for days before the sea came to look at it.

Ought she to be here? No one had ever said she must not come; people often sneaked back in the first days of the new year to see what had been taken and what had been left. But she was alone.

The rocks loomed about her, very dark on their shadowed side. Stars were already beginning to show above the peak of the island, although the sun still shone on it.

She started to walk across the slab and as she reached the middle one of those rocks moved. She saw its black shoulders rise and fall; it was putting out an arm.

She stood paralysed with fear. She ought not to have come here. The sea had posted its own guard to watch the grave, something nameless, unknown, that would tear her apart for her trespass.

Then the rock raised its head, the arm grew a hand and the hand brushed the hair out of its eyes. It spoke to her.

'Dede?'

She had heard the voice only three times before, but it was strange enough for her to recognize the speaker at once: Ianto Morgan, the guest, using the name that everyone else had forgotten.

'What are you doing here?' She was furious; a precious moment, and he had ruined it.

'Is it forbidden?'

'I don't know.' He sounded anxious, afraid that he might have given offence. Well, he had offended her, so let him be anxious. 'It might be – for you.'

'No one said anything. I can go where I like so long as I report to the barracks at sunrise and sunset. How long have I got?'

She looked at the sun, bowling down to the rim of the world. 'Not long.'

'I won't stay if you want to be alone. I just wondered what was happening here. Did you want to leave something?'

'We already did.'

'What's it all about – if you don't mind telling me? I would have asked one of the others, but they were already paired off.'

She knew who he meant by 'the others'. It wouldn't have hurt one of them to break the rules and make him welcome. They stayed as they were, he sitting among the rocks, she standing in the middle of the slab. She still could not see his face.

'This is the last day of the year,' Demetria said. 'We say goodbye to it.'

'Sort of burying it, burying the past?'

'Yes, I suppose so.' She had not thought of it like that.

'And how do you bring in the new year? Parties? Fireworks?'

'We don't bring it in, it just comes. What's fireworks?'

Now he sounded puzzled. 'Exploding lights in the sky.'

'Shooting stars?'

'No, shooting stars are natural, people *make* fireworks. So, no fireworks, no celebrations?'

'Today was a holiday.'

'Yes, I saw you all whooping it up,' he said grimly. 'You people certainly know how to have a good time.'

'And tomorrow's a holiday, too, but that's because it's the seventh day anyway.'

'Don't your days have names?'

'Of course: Unday, Twoday, Thriday, Foursday, Fi'day, Sixaday, Senday.'

'Tomorrow's Senday then; the first day of the new year. Isn't that special? What happens tomorrow?'

'Nothing, I said.' What was he on about?

'So that's all you do, bury the old year and let the new one take care of itself? Those things you've all put there, are they for good luck?'

They weren't supposed to be, but she knew that no one ever neglected to leave a token, however small, and somehow she knew also that those personal treasures people slipped in were more than tokens. But what was it to do with him, 37250 Ianto Morgan?

'What did you give?' he asked.

'Mam gave a bottle.'

'What of, wine?'

'What's wine? Just a bottle. It has to be old, what you give. Mam gave it for all of us, but I found it. Tycho brought it – with the logs that day, you know. It was a good thing to give back.'

'Ah!' There was an odd sound of triumph in his voice, as though he had discovered something. If he had, she must have told him. She was talking too

58

much. 'So these are gifts to the sea. You have to keep it sweet?'

'Sweet?'

'Propitiate it, make offerings – as I said – for good luck.'

'I suppose so.'

'Do you think I ought to give it something?'

'I dunno.'

'Do the others?'

'What others?' She realized how sulky she sounded.

'Oh, Dede, you must have noticed. I'm not the only – what do you call us? Guests?'

'Politicals.'

'Mmm. Do you know what that means?'

'No.'

'Well, do they give anything?'

'I don't know. Why should they, they don't belong here. Anyway, you haven't got anything to give. Mam said. When we got the shed ready for you, I thought you'd need somewhere to put your things and she said you wouldn't have any things. Just the clothes you stood up in.'

'It's not quite that bad now. Come on, Dede, what shall I give?'

'It's too late now. It has to be done by sunset.'

'The guards told me that sunset is over when the last light's gone up there on the peak – or when the hooter sounds if the clouds are thick. I've still got time – think of something.'

He seemed to be turning it into a sort of game. Two could play at that.

'Give it a hair of your beard.'

'Dede! Was that a joke? From you? From any of you?'

'It's a game we play. You think of a gift and say, "I will give you a – a – oh, a coil of rope." Rope costs a lot, see, and the other person has to think of something that's worth less than a coil of rope, like an oar, then you have to think of something less than an oar, and you keep going like that until you can't think of anything worth nothing, so you say, "I'll give you a hair of my head," and the first person who says that loses.'

'What a miserable game!' he cried. 'But only to be expected,' he added. 'Unfortunately, I can't even give that – the hair of my beard, I mean. They sent me my money this morning and do you know the very first thing I did? I went down to the barber. He didn't much want to serve me, but it's not against the rules apparently.'

He stood up as he spoke and she saw his face for the first time in the fading light. The beard had gone. He was young – well, not old. How long his nose looked now.

Demetria said, 'You haven't got much chin,' but, of

course, he would know that from the glass at the barber's.

'Is that a compliment?' Now that he was standing he walked over to the grave and stood looking down at the mound. Nearby the sea sucked and gurgled at clefts in the rocks. 'So what happens to all of this now?'

'Nothing. It stays there until the sea takes it. See, the wind's getting up. The waves will be here soon. It all goes in the end, back to Tycho. Sometimes there's still things here in summer, but it all goes in the end.'

'I'd have thought the first tide would have cleared it out,' he said.

'Tide?'

He looked up at the peak again. Only the very tip was sunlit now, the white snow flushed pink, and he started to walk away from the grave, back towards the quay and the barracks.

'I forgot, you don't have them here, do you?'

She ran after him. 'What's a tide?'

'It's the level of the sea, rising and falling, twice a day. If you had a tide the water here would come up to perhaps as far as . . .' he paused and looked among the darkening rocks '. . . up to the top of the harbour wall at least, as far as the barracks perhaps. Higher in spring and autumn.'

She was horrified. 'Then where would it go, up the mountain?'

'No, it can only go so high, unless there's a surge.

Then it goes down again. Up and down, up and down, forever. No one can stop it. Isn't that wonderful? All the amazing feats of technology that man has accomplished – but he can't stop the tides.'

They were crossing the quay now. She tried to imagine the sea rising up, up, over the stones of the harbour wall, over the mole, into the school, the barracks, the bakery, the barber's.

'*We've* stopped it,' she said. 'That's why it's good to give things back to Tycho.'

'No, no,' he said. 'It's nothing to do with the currents; it's caused by the moon.'

'The *moon*?'

'The pull of its gravity drags the sea.'

'No, it doesn't. The moon doesn't do anything. Look! It's rising now.'

From their eye level the sun was already set. The hooter had sounded. In the cold cloudless sky, blue-green like the sea on still mornings, a pale faltering light could be seen across the strait, just above the horizon.

'Where?'

She pointed. 'You'll see it better when it gets right dark.'

'That little tumbling rock?' He laughed bitterly in the almost-darkness. 'Call that a moon?'

Part Two

6

What other kind of a moon could there be? She lay in bed watching it, the little tumbling rock that flickered hesitantly as it climbed across the stars until it was hidden behind the lighthouse. Perhaps she would be asleep before it came out again on the other side.

It was not that small really. Somewhere she remembered learning that in truth it was as big as their own island, although she did not know how big that was, and much the same shape, with peaks and hollows, deeply pitted so that its surface caught the sunlight irregularly as it went spinning through the sky around the world. Before that she had believed the old story that once the island had been a twin moon that fell from the sky into the sea.

What had he meant, *Call that a moon?* There had been no time to ask him, for as he had said it the light had faded from the peak. He had run up the steps to the barracks and vanished inside the gate, and she had realized that she ought to be at home. It would be quite dark before she reached it; she had never been away from the house after nightfall before. There was enough afterglow to show her the way home, enough to show her Bevis coming down the street to meet her, fastening his hand round her arm and dragging her the last few metres as though he had arrested her.

'Skulking about outside,' he said, delivering her into the kitchen. Supper was on the table.

'I wasn't skulking. I was coming home. I was running.'

'Who said you could stay out this late?'

'No one said I couldn't.'

'That's enough of your lip.' He flipped her across the mouth. Mam went on spooning stew out of the saucepan into bowls. Demetria knew better than to appeal to her.

Lying there in bed, later, waiting for the moon to reappear from behind the lighthouse, she tried to remember if Mam had said anything about being home earlier. Mam said so little it was unlikely that Demetria would have forgotten.

The silent darkness was ripped apart by a strident shriek that rose and fell and rose again. Even from five kilometres away, even through the stone walls of the house, the noise shocked her into sitting upright. Before the howl reached its second peak the light-house beam went out, but the howl went on and on.

What must it sound like over there on the Low Island where it was right on top of you?

She knelt on the bed and looked out of the window, but she could not see the strait from here. Her bed was not in a proper room but in an alcove at the top of the stairs, without a door. It was understood that when the Banshee raised her voice people stayed indoors, in their rooms. Mam and Bevis would not stir, but what of Ianto Morgan? Had he been warned about the Banshee or would he go running outside, down to the harbour even, to find out what was happening? He was not locked in now.

Something that she had been trying not to remember nudged her conscience. Once, the night had not ended only with shots from the island – there had been one closer, louder, on their side of the strait. She never knew who the shot had been aimed at, or if it had found its mark. No one she knew of had been killed or wounded. There had been no funeral that she knew about, up on the hillside below the lighthouse. No one said anything. Could it have been a Political?

It was none of her business if Ianto Morgan went out and got himself shot. She almost wished he had remained an anonymous number, nothing to worry about; now he had a name he was flesh and blood, particularly blood.

The two doors along the narrow slip of passage remained closed. Mam and Bevis were not coming out; they might even sleep through the Banshee's clamour; some people could. Demetria slid from the bed and was on the stairs in the same movement. The house was utterly dark, but there were only ten steps down. The third and the ninth creaked. Mam might sleep through the Banshee but not the creaking. Counting, Demetria avoided them and ran noiselessly over the cold stone floor of the kitchen to the end window.

By the starlight she saw that the door of the shed was open. He had come out. Then she saw him. The seaward wall of the garden was too high to see over. He was opening the gate to the road.

Don't go out. Don't go out, she begged silently. He stood framed in the gateway, staring out across the hillside to the sea. She knew what he was looking at; the other window at the front showed her the same view: the cluster of blazing lights on the horizon and the swinging boom of a searchlight raking the wave-caps in the strait. And the Banshee blared on.

She glanced back to the garden. The gateway was empty, the gate still open. He was on the road.

Mam's room was over the kitchen; the head of Bevis's bed must be exactly above the street door. She could not get out without alerting one or the other, but now Ianto Morgan was walking, drawing level with the front window. He was not moving very fast, and he stopped; he had wanted a better view, that was all. The windows were sealed shut for the winter –

how could she attract his attention? If she tapped on the glass he would never hear that timid sound beneath the Banshee's braying, and now he was walking on again.

Her sweating palms were pressed against the pane. The right one slipped, letting out a tiny screech as it skidded on the glass. Either he heard it, miraculously, or he caught the movement out of the tail of his eye. His head came round. There was only starlight above them, but he was close enough to see her, to see something, on the other side of the window; not her face, perhaps, but the two splayed hands. He came close. She mouthed, 'Go back, go back, go inside,' and made frantic jabs with her finger to show him the way he must go.

He understood and started to turn back. Then he reached up and laid his own palm gently against the glass where her face was pressed to it.

Thank you.

Standing well back in the middle of the room, she watched through the end window until she saw the gate shut, a shadow on the path and then the closing of the shed door.

She was so relieved that as she went back up the stairs she forgot about the creaking ninth. She fled up the rest, leaping over the third, and was in bed again before Mam's door had opened.

She lay with her face to the wall, feeling her

mother standing at the head of the stairs. Finally she spoke.

'Have you been out of bed?'

Demetria rolled over with a start. 'I didn't know you were there.'

Whatever Bevis had said, she had never been a liar as Mam knew perfectly well, even if she chose to think otherwise, so this lie was believed. Neither of them mentioned the Banshee.

'I thought I heard someone on the stairs.'

'I didn't hear.'

Mam went down a few steps, peered and came up again. The door of her room closed behind her. Demetria knelt up on the bed again and looked out of the window. The moon was out of sight now, but the lighthouse remained unlit and the Banshee wailed until dawn.

'See you tomorrow,' she had said to Stephane as they had parted yesterday evening. The day stretched emptily before her. There was no need to go looking for Stephane, they were sure to run into each other sooner or later, at the market, on the beach.

Demetria turned from the street at the stooping thorn tree and took the path down to the shore. The wind was brisk and cold this morning, rattling the dry winter grass in the fields on the landward side of the path. There was rain in it; over on her right the super-structure of the Low Island was shrouded in murk. At breakfast no one had spoken of the Banshee's cry in the night, the night that had not ended in shots. Mam had taken Ianto Morgan his breakfast before she went to market, since there was no longer any need to wait for the soldier to unlock the shed. Looking down the path in the half-light Demetria saw him open the shed door and take the tray. He said thank you; she saw his lips form the words. Mam did not answer, she had already turned and was walking back to the house, although he was still speaking. Ianto Morgan shrugged and closed the door.

He must have been asking a question, about last night perhaps. He would know better than to do that again. Later he had returned the tray and the kettle, taking advantage of his freedom to do that. Mam had already left. Bevis went to the door, scowling.

'It's no trouble,' Demetria heard Ianto Morgan say. 'The bell has just sounded off. I've fifteen minutes, I'm told, to get down to the barracks, to report.'

'You don't come to the house,' Bevis said. 'Leave the tray on the step as you did before.'

Bevis was easily young enough to be his son, but he spoke to the Political as he never would have dared to an island man. It would have fetched him a clout round the ear.

'Shall I take it back then?' Ianto Morgan said. There was that ripple in his voice that she remembered from yesterday, as if he were trying not to laugh although there was nothing to laugh at. Bevis had snatched the tray and the kettle, kicking the door shut behind him. They had not seen the Political since – he must be down in the town now. Perhaps he had gone back to look at the grave, and she thought, rather sadly, that he never had put anything in it. She hoped he would have the sense not to touch it; probably he had noticed the waves in the strait and wanted to watch the sea claiming its own.

The water was choppy, smashing against the mole and sending up explosions of spray. On the beach the waves curled and crashed; the crescent of sand was much narrower than on the day the logs had come in. There was no one else there yet, but if the sea kept up this pounding other children were sure to come along and see if it were bringing anything. Till then it was all hers.

She dreamed of finding a shell like the one she had seen put into the grave, whole and perfect as if someone had carved it by hand from white ice, as big as a gourd, but most shells that made it to land were small black hemispheres, thick and indestructable. The rest were hurled ashore in fragments.

Then she saw it, rolling in the surf a few metres out – a lone log, not very thick or very long, hardly even a dolphin, but hers for the taking if she could reach it; such a prize to bear home alone. She threw off her coat in spite of the cold, untied her knitting bag which must never get wet, rolled up her trouser legs and tucked her skirt into her waistband. If she should lose her footing the heavy clothes would drag her down.

The log was bucking and dipping, temptingly close now, but still it might not beach itself. She could see that it was not one of the usual kind, not a trunk or even part of a trunk, but perhaps a lopped branch, and instead of being cylindrical it had bits sticking up out of it, almost like handles. She would not have to clasp it bodily and manhandle it to shore; if she could just grab one of those handles she could tow it in.

The water was over her knees, over her trousers. Her skirt was draggling in the foam as she tried to reach the log and dodge the waves at the same time, but her fingers closed round wood and the log turned obediently towards her.

In the shallows it became heavy and unwieldy, wallowing and dragging in her hands. She stooped and rolled it now, out of the surf, up the sand.

A flat voice said, 'That's ours.'

She looked up. Two of the Coveney brothers were standing in the path of the log. A third, the smallest, hardly more than a toddler, was waddling insecurely towards them across the beach.

'Get your hands off it,' Brodie Coveney said. 'We saw it first.'

'No – I was here. I got it out myself.'

'We *saw* it first.' Brendan's voice was just as toneless. He was not expecting an argument. 'We were on our way down to fetch it when you barged in.'

She knew it was hopeless but this was her first log, her own; she had won it. 'I was down here before you. I saw it. I went in and got it.' Over Brodie's shoulder she saw a man approaching from the direction of the harbour. That would be the end of the matter – the Coveneys would simply take the log because they and the man would be on the same side, but in a sudden rush of defiance she clung to her prize.

'Why should you have it? I went in and got it.'

Brodie simply aimed his fist at her head. Brendan put out his hand and shoved and she went over, rolling in the foam, but even as she fell she heard a shout and saw the man start running.

She scrambled upright as he reached them and she saw it was Ianto Morgan. He looked angry, astounded.

'Leave her alone.'

Equally astounded, Brendan and Brodie turned to face him.

'What are you doing?' Ianto Morgan said. 'That's Dede's log. I saw her go in after it.'

They stared at him. Demetria wished he had not called her Dede. No one used that name now; she did not want the Coveneys to know that anyone had ever used it.

'We saw it first,' Brendan started to say, but Brodie cut in.

'It's one of *them*. Take no notice. He can't do anything.' He saw Demetria on her feet and, looking Ianto Morgan coldly in the eye, pushed her down again.

'You miserable bullies, you dreary little thugs,' Ianto Morgan said. He seemed hardly able to get the words out. Didn't he understand? 'Too slow to fetch out your own driftwood, so you beat up a little girl and steal hers.'

'They have to learn,' Brodie said.

'Learn what?'

He was like that other Political yesterday who had been shocked when Audrey's brother hit her. They didn't understand. Taylor Coveney, the littlest one, had caught up now, eager to join in. He lurched towards Demetria, landed a slap on her bare leg and overbalanced, sitting down hard in the water. His mouth opened in an outraged howl.

'Serves you right, you horrible brat,' Ianto Morgan said. He took a step forward. Brodie skipped out of his way, but he had his fists up.

'You don't touch us,' he said. 'Don't you know we could have you shot?'

He and Brendan picked up the log between them and started up the beach as if there were no more to be said, Taylor floundering and grizzling in their wake. Ianto Morgan stood watching them go, his own fists clenched. Demetria could see that he was itching to lay into them.

'Is that it?' he said at last. 'Is this how things are?'

Demetria shook her skirt loose and rolled down her trouser legs. She could not bear to pull her stockings up over cold, wet skin, but she shuffled into her shoes.

'Why do you stand for it?' he said. 'What did he mean, "They have to learn"?'

She recited for him: 'A man may beat his own wife but not another man's wife. A brother may beat his sister but not the sister of another.'

He looked sick. 'They aren't your brothers.'

'No, a brother should defend his sister . . . but they're all each other's brothers really.'

'So, while you are children your brothers are allowed to knock you about so that you get used to it before you become women and your husbands start on you?'

The Coveneys had reached the bend in the path now. She could still hear Taylor's wailing. She thought of what Ianto Morgan had said as they started to walk away with their log, her log.

'That's how things are.'

7

She hoped that he would go away, but he stayed where he was, looking from her to the Coveneys, who were almost out of sight, and back to her again.

'I should have thrashed them,' he said, 'but it wouldn't have done any good, would it?'

'It wouldn't have done *you* any good. Can they really have you shot?'

'I don't think so. If I were going to be shot it would have happened already – I wouldn't have been sent here – but that's not what I meant. I haven't made things any easier for you, have I? I should have stayed out of it altogether.'

She almost said 'yes', but she was remembering that astonishment, that hope, she had felt when she realized that the man coming along the beach towards them was on *her* side, not theirs; that he would try to stop them. He had *defended* her; tried to. That was what the word meant, that thing a brother or a father was supposed to do – to step in, to stand between, to stop the blows falling – unless they were his blows.

'This learning business,' Ianto Morgan said, 'these awful things you learn. Where do you learn them?'

'At school.'

'Oh god,' he groaned. He really did groan, as if he had a pain. 'So no one hits you till you go to school, till you're taught to hurt and be hurt?'

'No, of course not. I mean, yes. You get hit, but at school they teach you the rules.'

'Written down, are they, these rules? Tablets of stone?'

'No. There's a big board at the front and Teacher writes on it and we copy things down. That's how we learn how to write.'

'And does no one think it's wrong?'

'But it isn't. It's the rules.'

'Do you think it's right then? You're on the receiving end.'

'It's the—'

'All right,' he said, 'I heard you. Let's walk, Dede. You shouldn't be standing around in wet clothes in this wind. Put your coat on, quick. Walk up and down a bit. What else do they teach you in this school of yours?'

'Knitting,' Demetria said.

'All of you?'

'The girls. That's what we do when we're grown

up, see. We all learn to read and write and reckon figures and weights – we have to know those. Then we make a bag –' she held out hers as she tied it round her waist again – 'and that's to keep our knitting in. Then we learn to knit.'

'I thought it was an apron.'

'No, it opens, look. We have to take care of it because it's the one we keep till we get married.' She recalled how proud she had been, making that bag and tying it on for the first time. 'Then we have a special bag – it's given as a wedding present. We wear them all the time.'

'So I've noticed,' he said, sounding displeased.

'Yes, well, when the girls start knitting the boys learn the drifts, in case they're going to work on the boats, and net-making and how to work wood, those sorts of things.'

'And the girls learn to knit. What do you knit?'

'Everything,' Demetria said. 'Stockings, sweaters, gloves, hats, scarves – all our clothes except for cloth things.' She clutched a fold of damp skirt. 'Cloth comes on the mail-boats.'

'Where does it come from?'

'I don't know. Somewhere over there.' She pointed to the horizon.

'Where the logs come from?'

'I don't know where the logs come from. We buy cloth in the market, and sell the knitting. Mam's there now; she does seamen's stockings and gloves. I'm learning stockings now. I hate stockings, turning heels. I'm no good at it, but Mam says stockings is what we do.'

'And what does Dad say?'

'I haven't got a dad. Didn't you know? There's only us, me and Mam and Bevis.'

'I assumed he was out on the boats – I mean – I don't know who lives in your house. I've not been in it, have I? I'm sorry, Dede. What happened to him?'

'Kepler took him, before I was born.'

They had reached the Point. At the other end of the beach figures were appearing over the rocks from the harbour.

'Isn't there anywhere else to go in this godforsaken place? What's on the other side of these cliffs?'

'More cliffs, all the way round. We could walk across the fields, over there, you know, where the path is.' Clearly she was not going to get rid of him.

'Let's walk across the fields then.'

They turned alongside the grassy flank of the cliff, then crossed the sandy scrub that rose steeply until it was cut off by the wall where the enclosed fields began.

'Stop here a moment, will you?' Ianto Morgan said. He leaned against the wall, breathing hard, almost wheezing.

'What's the matter?' She had never known anyone get out of breath so fast, not just by walking.

'I find your air a little thin,' he said faintly. Demetria wondered if he were perhaps mad. People were thin. How could air be thin?

After a few moments he straightened up and walked on. 'When I came to find you on the beach—' he began.

'How did you know I'd be on the beach?'

'I didn't know. After I came out of the barracks I looked around the market and then I went for a walk on the mole, until the soldiers turned me back. That was when I saw you, going in after your log. Now, if you had tides, they would bring the logs in for you. I didn't know it was you at first, but I wanted to thank you properly for what you did last night. I could have got into bad trouble. Did you guess I'd go out?'

'When you heard the Banshee? Yes, I thought you mightn't know . . . that you shouldn't.'

'Is that what you call it, the Banshee? Very apt.'

'What?'

'It's a good name for such an unholy racket.'

She did not know what he was talking about. 'That's not its name, that's what it is. It means someone's tried to escape from the Low Island – where the lights are, didn't you see? And when it sounds, they have to put out our lighthouse.' She was telling him things that islanders never mentioned, even to each other. 'See, the only way off the Low Island is through the sea to this one. If a light was showing, they'd know the way.'

'Aren't there any other lights?'

'Curfew's an hour after sunset. You have to put out the lights or have the shutters up. Haven't you got a light?'

'I'm saving up for an oil lamp,' he said.

'You'll have to cover the louvres.' Someone should have told him that, she thought vaguely. Mam . . .

'So they're left to drown, are they, these poor beggers in the sea?'

'If they aren't shot.'

'It's an even better name than I thought,' he said. 'Do you know what a Banshee is?'

'The noise –'

'The Banshee was a fairy woman who wailed under the windows of a house when someone was going to die.'

'What's a ferry woman?'

Ianto Morgan stopped walking and stared at her. She stopped too.

'You don't know about fairies? You don't have fairy tales?'

'What are they?'

'No songs?'

'What's a song?'

He had no control over his face, she could see everything he was thinking. Then he began to speak, but his voice was all over the place, rising and falling, almost like the Banshee, only the Banshee spoke no words. Demetria supposed they were words that he was using, but they were not like any words she had ever heard.

He stopped. 'That's a song, *Ar Hyd y Nos*. That's singing.'

'What's it mean?'

'"All Through the Night" – in Welsh.'

'What's Welsh?'

'It's another language – other kinds of words. It isn't spoken here.'

'What's it for?'

'Welsh?'

'Singing.'

'Oh my god.' Now he whispered. 'You've never heard a song before? Not even a lullaby when you were a baby?'

'What's—'

'A song for little children, to send them to sleep.'

'You don't get sent to sleep, you just go. Oh – you get sent to *bed*.'

'No lullabies, no songs. No stories. You learn to be beaten, you celebrate the new year by holding a funeral. Why am I here? Why do you think I'm here? Oh Dede, I must have done something very terrible, don't you think, to be sent here.'

'No. If you'd done something terrible you'd be on the Low Island.'

'What happened? How did you all get like this? You must have had something once or you wouldn't have that word.'

'What word?' She was growing afraid. He had fallen to his knees in the grass, clutching his arms across his chest as though the thing that had made him groan was a real, griping pain.

'Is the air too thin again?'

'Banshee. That word came from somewhere, it couldn't have come alone. What happened to the rest? Where has it all gone?'

She almost thought he was crying, not as Taylor Coveney had cried, loud abandoned bawling, but a silent shaking. He was ashamed and bowed his head. Really frightened now she began to run, up the hill, across the fields, over walls, towards home where nothing was new or strange.

In school next morning it seemed that nothing had changed there either. The bare walls, the high, wide windows, were the same. The windows were on the seaward side to catch the best of the light as the sun moved round, but just too high to see out of unless you were on tiptoe.

The teacher stood where she always stood unless she was checking on their work; everyone was in her usual seat, Demetria in the fifth row back, next to the aisle, Stephane beside her. There was a subdued murmur of conversation. They were allowed to talk while they knitted, but only once they had mastered the particular task they had been set. This was hard on Stephane who was an accomplished knitter, nearing the toe of another completed stocking and stuck next to silent Demetria who was still on heels, endless heels, to be repeated over and over again until she could make a smooth turn.

Only practice would do it, and dried peas. If you handed in a heel with cobbles or knotted yarn you had to put dried peas in the heels of your own stockings for the rest of the day to remind you how it would feel to the person who had to wear your work. She had them in her stockings now, which was why she had eased her feet out of her shoes, hoping that Teacher would not notice. This too was the same, it had been going on for weeks; she knew that she would never learn to turn a heel.

But something was different. There was the muffled sawing and hammering from the next room where the boys worked at their carpentry, the quiet voices in this one, the clicking needles, the heavy tread of Teacher's shoes as she walked up and down the aisles. Everything was as usual, but under it she heard something new, the unsettling voice that went up and down, hanging on to words and making them climb and slide. She could not remember those words, they had not sounded like any words she had heard before, but she remembered the effect and she wanted to hear it again; singing.

How was it done? His voice had come out much deeper than when he spoke. Could she do it? She

85

might try, but not here, not now. She was not even allowed to speak.

Teacher was beside her, a hand held out for her work. Demetria passed over the thick grey web on its four needles and waited for the inevitable comment: *That won't do. Go back and start again.*

It was never enough to go back to whatever mistake she had made. Under Teacher's eye she would have to pull out the needles and unravel the knitting back to the first stitch. She waited.

'Well, right at last,' Teacher said. Demetria looked up. Teacher did not smile but she was not frowning either. 'Do one more, to make sure you have it perfect, and then you may carry on to the toe.'

She had begun to despair of ever reaching a toe.

'May I take the peas out, please?'

Teacher paused. 'No, keep them in until you go home, they'll remind you to pay attention. And I don't want to hear you talking until you've done that next heel and got it right again. No excuse for mistakes now, I know you can do it.'

This was almost praise. Demetria cast off the heel, laid it on her table where she could see it, and cast on another. If she could manage this one as well, she might reach the toe by the end of the afternoon. Toes had to be smooth and flawless too – she would be sure to find herself in trouble with them – but till then there was only one more heel and then a lovely straight run down the foot.

Across the room Audrey was working on one of the thick sweaters the fishermen wore that came down almost to the knees, with long necks that rolled over. They were heavy and hard work, but not difficult once you had learned to set the sleeves, not like stockings. Demetria would have far rather worked on sweaters, but her family did stockings and gloves, they always had. It was just bad luck that these were the most complicated garments. Her only hope of escape was to marry into a family that did scarves and hats, like Josephine's, but Josephine had no brothers.

Because they took on the work of their husbands' families, they all had to learn to knit everything before specializing in the clothes they would knit as unmarried women, still wearing their old school knitting bags. The Coveney women did scarves and hats – could she bear to marry a Coveney? Would any Coveney want her? Stephane's brother, Devlin, was the only boy she could imagine growing into a kindly man, but Stephane's family did stockings too.

Was there no other way out? She had dropped a stitch, two rows down. Hiding from Teacher's eye behind Stephane she took a spare needle and hooked it up. Teacher knitted all the time as she walked, as women were supposed to do, beautiful complex patterns and colours that were never seen on the island. They all went away on the mail-boats to be sold on the mainland. Teacher's husband was quite a wealthy man because of those beautiful patterns.

That might be a different future, teaching; but not for her. Teacher had got the job because she was an expert knitter. Her reading and writing were not much better than Demetria's, but then they did not need to be.

There went another stitch. She must stop thinking of anything but the knitting. That was what they were told, *Don't think*. In the end they would be so proficient that they would be able to think, talk, even read while they knitted, as if anyone would do such a thing, but that time was a long way off – it might never come for Demetria. She firmly pushed everything out of her mind except for the knitting, and the maddening persistent memory of that strange sound Ianto Morgan had called singing.

At dinner break a quick game of hop-toad got under way. Demetria did not join in because of the peas. She sat on the wall and Stephane joined her, looking down over the harbour. The boats were out today; there was not much going on at the quayside. The soldiers were having their dinner break too, lounging in the yard of the barracks on the mole. On the far side of the quay, where the rocks began, a little group of Politicals was standing, talking. *He* was there. It was the first time she had seen him with anyone else.

'They shouldn't be doing that,' Stephane said, 'not three of them.'

'But they aren't doing anything,' Demetria said. 'Just standing.'

'They're talking. Don't you know anything?'

Demetria did know. She had been hoping no one would notice the men. 'They're allowed to talk.'

'Not three. That's the rules. Never more than two together. Three's a conspiracy.'

'What *is* a conspiracy?'

'I don't know. Three Politicals talking.'

Stephane was not the only one who had seen them. One of the boys was yelling for the Master. 'Sir! Sir! Conspiracy!'

Others took up the cry: 'Conspiracy! Conspiracy!'

The soldiers heard. A couple of them strolled over to the wall to look, and by now the whole of the boys' class was shouting. Some of the girls joined in but they were soon slapped into silence. The word bounced back at them from walls and rocks: '*Conspiracy!*'

The men had taken the hint and split up, two walking in one direction, one in another. The soldiers, satisfied, returned to their dinners and tobacco. The boys, who had hoped for more action, continued to yell, but they had got what they wanted. The little group was dispersed.

Why should they care? Demetria thought. What's it to them if those men talk to each other? But she remembered the scene on Old Year's Day, when the brothers had broken up the hop-toad game and the Politicals had wanted to intervene.

'One of them must be new,' Stephane said. 'You've got a new Political, haven't you? Was it yours?'

'Dunno. Couldn't see. They all look the same,' Demetria muttered. But that must be what had happened; Ianto Morgan learning the hard way to remember the rules. Perhaps he had thought it safe to break them with only schoolchildren watching. He had been left to learn everything the hard way, come to think of it. The boy who had raised the cry of conspiracy was Brodie Coveney, getting his own back for the scene on the beach yesterday. He might not be able to have a man shot but he wanted revenge for those three strange words that Ianto Morgan had called him and his brothers: *thug*; *bully*; *brat*.

She had never heard them before but she knew what they meant in the mouth of a man who hadn't understood how things were. Thug, bully, brat; hard words, the sounds of punching, shoving, slapping.

Thug. Bully. Brat.

8

The biggest buildings on the landward side of the quay were the fish-packing plant and the smokery, the woollen mill, where the herders brought their fleeces in summer, and the saw mill. In a row in front of them stood the town shops – bakery, dairy, general store, the tavern and the barber's – men's places, next to each other, and, most important of all, Donald the chandler, where the boatmen bought their gear. Anything else you might need was sold in the market. Miss that and you went without for another week.

Mam and Stephane's mam, and other women, were selling their knitting and knitting as they sold, at the stalls on the quayside under awnings that snapped and tugged in the wind. Demetria was shopping for yarn and thread, potatoes and flour from the store, and oil from the chandler's. The oilcan was heavy. Carrying fuel was officially held to be men's work and, if they were big enough, boys' work. Bevis usually fetched the oil but today he had given the job to Demetria after hearing she had been seen in the fields, talking to a Political.

He did not know it was their own Political. People tended not to know the strangers' names and they were hard to tell apart. But they were easily recognized for what they were, Ianto Morgan included, because of the way they dressed, like mainlanders, in shirts and long coats instead of sweaters and reefers, and by their skins, pale from lack of exposure to the elements, and their hair. On the whole it was much darker than island hair – bark-coloured, shading to black like Ianto Morgan's. Even the fair ones did not have that bleached-to-whiteness look of the islanders. But someone had seen her with a Political and word had got back to Bevis. It must have been a Coveney.

She had not seen Ianto Morgan for two weeks now – had word got to him too? Mam continued to take his meals to him twice a day. Since he had discovered how heavy the iron kettle was he had offered to carry it himself, but she refused. She did not want him even as close as the doorstep.

And now, here he was, in the chandler's, buying soap and candles – he must have been told how much lamp-oil would cost him. Demetria withdrew into a corner behind hanging skeins of rope. The chandler's also served as a post office. Mail could be left there and collected, once the censor had been through it.

The censor had appeared at about the time of the first Politicals, an old man from the mainland who lodged at the lighthouse and came down on the day before the mail-boat was due, to go through the letters that were being sent out, and again, the next day, to examine incoming mail. Demetria had no idea what he did with it. Very few islanders sent letters to the mainland, or received them.

Ianto Morgan was asking for paper and envelopes. Donald, moving behind the counter to become post-master, handed him a pack of small pale-blue cards.

'You have to use these.'

'No envelopes?'

'Your kind have to use cards, weren't you told? Of course you were – no sealed mail. Don't try it on with me.'

'I thought that meant we had to leave the envelopes unsealed.'

'Did you now? Well, you were wrong. Do you want these or not?'

Ianto Morgan paid for his cards and went away without saying anything else. Demetria waited until he was outside again before emerging from behind the rope with her oilcan. Donald was never a friendly man, even with the locals. She had heard him deal with Politicals before, in the hostile voice he kept especially for them.

As she was lugging the can and the shopping up the hill she heard footsteps on the stones behind her and

Ianto Morgan drew level. He held out his hand for the oilcan, as he had done for the sack of bark that time on log-fall day.

'Let me carry that.'

Who might be watching? But her fingers were already stiffening round the handle. She let him take it.

'God almighty,' he said, half to himself. 'Wood stoves and oil lamps. No wonder you pray for those logs – and they won't last for ever at the rate they're going. What'll you do then? What became of your electricity?'

'What's that?'

Apparently lost for words he walked on for a while before answering. 'It's a kind of fuel. You must have had a turbine here once, some kind of a generator. That lighthouse can't burn oil or wood, they'd never be able to turn it off so fast. I bet they've got a generator. Isn't there a turbine up on the mountain? With all this wind you could power a city.' With the steep climb and his furious muttering he was out of breath again. He gasped, 'Does it never stop blowing?'

'In summer, sometimes. What's a generator?'

He started to answer but cut himself off with a sigh. 'Life's too short. Is this your regular job?'

'Shopping?'

'Carrying the oil.'

'No, Bevis does it.'

'Injured himself, has he? Or were you sorry for the

poor, weak, little fellow having to haul this heavy burden?'

There he went again, that thing that happened to his voice when he said something he did not mean. It had the opposite effect on her, making her say exactly what she meant.

'No, someone saw me talking to you in the fields that time, and he said if I carried the oil he wouldn't tell Mam.'

'Blackmail.'

'No, mail's white. Yours is blue, I saw you buying it.'

'Blackmail isn't precisely letters,' he said. 'It's more a way of making people do what you want. "You do this or I'll do that." Your mother wouldn't like me talking to you?'

Mam did not much like her talking to anyone, as far as she could see, but especially not to him. She felt the first faint stirring of resentment, although she did not know what it was. This was the one person she knew, apart from Stephane, who really wanted to talk to her, and she was not supposed to talk to him.

'Where's the brother now?'

'Out on the rocks, getting pillocks.'

'What are they?'

'Little fish in shells, for bait. Those round black things on the beach, those are pillock shells.'

'And your mam's at the market?'

'How did you know?'

'I saw her while I was buying this.' He pulled aside his coat and she saw that he was wearing a blue sweater under it, over his shirt. It looked funny like that, with the collar showing. 'Warm at last,' he said.

'That's Audrey's; she knitted it. She's still at school, but her mam sells her work already. I hope she marries into a sweater family. It would be a shame if she ended up just doing scarves. I'd like to do scarves, I'm no good at stockings,' Demetria said.

'Why shouldn't she go on knitting sweaters when she marries?' Like many of his questions, the answer was obvious; the questions she could answer, that was.

'When you get married you knit what your husband's family knits.'

'Even if you're brilliant at sweaters, like Audrey? Suppose you want to go on knitting sweaters?'

'Oh no, you have to change,' Demetria said.

'And what happens if all the sweater knitters marry out? Will you have to run around in scarves and stockings? What happens if you don't like knitting at all?'

'I don't like knitting,' Demetria said, 'but that's what we do.'

They had reached the garden gate. He opened it for her and stood aside while she went in ahead of him. She got the impression that he thought it was the right thing to do.

'Where will I put the oil?'

'In the outhouse – there with the logs.' She opened the kitchen door. 'You can't come in.'

'I know that. Will you come out?'

'Out where?'

'Here in the garden. It's sheltered on this side of the wall.'

'What for?'

'To talk. I ought to apologize. I upset you the other day.'

She came out again and sat on the step in the sunshine. He hunkered down with his back against the wall. 'Was it my singing?'

'What?'

'That upset you.'

'No.' It had been his own grief. 'I didn't understand. "Where's it all gone?" you said. Where's what gone?'

'Everything.' He groaned again. 'Laughter, kindness, good fellowship, music, stories . . . electricity.'

'We have stories,' Demetria said.

'Have you? Tell me one of your stories.'

She thought about it. 'They told us this one at school,' she said. 'When we're little they tell us stories while we learn to knit.'

'Don't the little boys get stories while they learn to saw?'

'I don't know – they wouldn't be able to hear them, would they? This is a girls' story. It's the story of the little mermaid.'

'You know that?' He seemed astonished. 'How she rescues a prince from drowning and falls in love – that story?'

'No. What's a prince? The little mermaid – that's a thing that lives in the sea and one end of it's a fishtail – this mermaid gets caught in a fisherman's net, but she's too small to eat so he throws her back, but she wants to be his wife, so she asks an old merwoman how to make him marry her and she does all the things this old merwoman says, and then next time the fisherman comes out she swims into his net on purpose, and she's so beautiful he asks her to marry him and she does, but when he finds out she isn't any good he swings her round by the tail and dashes her brains out and gives her to the fishwives, and they put her on a slab and cut her open and they see she has only got a fish heart after all, so they gut her and make her into soup.'

She saw his look of horror.

'They *had* to. She wasn't any good, you see; she couldn't knit. Don't be upset, it's only a story. Those mermaids aren't real.'

'It's a true story, though, isn't it?' he said after a very long silence. 'Dede, what's in this world of yours, apart from the island?'

'Well, the Low Island of course. We can see that. And the mainland – over there. It's a long way off.'

'*The* mainland. Is that the only other land, do you think? In all this world, just these two islands and the mainland? How big is the mainland? How far does it go? Where does it stop?'

'It doesn't stop.'

'Then where does the sea start?'

'I don't know.'

'If you got into a boat and sailed away, following Tycho, where would it take you? You know this world's a sphere, don't you? Like a ball.'

'Of course. Otherwise we'd be able to see forever.'

'So what's beyond the mainland? Do you know?'

'Do you?'

'There are other mainlands,' he said, 'other islands. Three great mainlands, thousands of islands.'

'Have you been there? Have you seen them?'

'I've seen maps. Have you ever seen a map?'

'There are maps in the boys' room at school, so they can learn the shoals and drifts. They're all covered in little arrows, like fish swimming. And we're in the middle. But there's no mainlands on them, just High Island and Low Island.'

'So how did you get here?'

'I was born.'

'No, how did people come to be living on these islands? Did they swim here, do you think; crawl out of the seas like merpeople and grow legs and live on land?'

She laughed. '*No.*'

'Did they fly?'

'What's fly?'

There was another silence, even longer.

'If I told you I flew here, you wouldn't know what I meant?'

'Didn't you come on the mail-boat like the others?'

'Yes, to the island . . . Dede, have you got work to do?'

'It's Senday. I've done all my work; there's no school.'

'And your mam's in the market and your charming brother is collecting pillocks – how apt. Will you come down to the beach?'

'To see what Tycho's brought?'

'We might, but I want to show you something. I need pebbles.'

'All right. But I must put the shopping away.'

'Even better. I'll go down now. Then we can just meet, on the shore.'

'We'll be seen.'

'Ah, yes, the blackmail. Is it forbidden by law for us to talk? I know we – people like me – are sent here because no one will talk to us; I can see why now. They don't even talk to each other. Even you children – I've watched you, you've got nothing to say. You don't know anything – no, sorry, I didn't mean to insult you. But children like to talk usually. Mine do.'

He was still outside. Demetria had taken the shopping into the kitchen and was sorting foodstuffs from needlework, on the table. She left it and came back to the door.

'Have you got children?'

'Three.'

'Where are they?'

'Well . . . I had to leave them behind. We're not allowed to bring our families with us when we come here, and mine is a long way away. A very long way.' He turned from her abruptly and stood up, heading for the gate. 'Come down when you're ready. It's still quite early, we should have the beach to ourselves for a while. If Tycho brings me anything I'll save it for you.' He paused and came back, but stayed off the step. 'Can't you take off that damned bag?'

'No, we never take them off outdoors. See, when we grow up we can knit at any time, just walking about.'

'It's like some ghastly slave collar,' he said. 'Oh god, that was another insult, wasn't it? Do you know where Tycho and Kepler get their names from?' He did not wait for an answer; he knew she would not have one. 'They were astronomers, men who studied the stars. If it weren't for them you wouldn't be here.'

'Why not?'

'I mean, you wouldn't be *here*.'

She thought he was going to say more, but when she looked round again he had gone.

9

As on most market mornings the beach was empty. The Coveneys were probably gathering pillocks on the rocks below the sea grave. Stephane might be wondering where Demetria had got to but she had not come looking for her here.

Ianto Morgan was kneeling at the cliff's foot, on a little patch of sand, but as she came down the path she had seen him wandering along the shore line, picking things up.

Now he was making patterns in the sand with pebbles. As she reached him he looked up and pointed to the one in front of him. Her eye wandered to another, a little further off – a set of concentric rings with a round white stone in the middle – but he pointed firmly at the nearer one.

'Pretend this is the world, this pebble,' he said. 'You know how to pretend, don't you? Or don't you?'

'Oh yes. The pattern is like a map. A map is a pretend place.'

'I suppose it is. Right, this is the sun. And this –' he tapped a smaller darker pebble beside it – 'this is your planet.'

'My planet?'

'Your world.'

'*My* world?'

'It's not the only world, Dede. And here, this scrap of shell – your moon.'

'The little tumbling rock?'

'Did I say that? Yes, that's it. And you know how these three work together? The world goes round the sun, and the moon goes round the world, all the time, spinning, spinning, through space. And you know the sun is a star, like all the other stars in the sky?'

'Is it?' She understood, this was a sort of game. She might as well learn to play it.

'Have they told you that some of those other stars have worlds spinning round them?'

'Do they?'

'Come over here,' he said, moving on hands and knees to the second, bigger pattern, the one that looked more interesting, with rings. 'Here's another sun, it's called Sol.' He laid his finger on the round white pebble.

'Is this another story?'

'No, this is real, this is true. This sun doesn't have

one planet spinning round it, it has nine; the system of Sol – solar system. Look, here they are. This one, nearest to the sun, is Mercury—'

'They've got names?'

'They've got names. Mercury, Venus, Earth, Mars, Jupiter, Saturn, Neptune, Uranus, Pluto. This big fellow, Jupiter, has dozens of moons. Saturn has thirty, Mars has two, like yours, little tumbling rocks, and this one, the third one, has a moon one quarter as big as itself, look. It hangs in the sky like another planet, a white planet, it's so close, and as it spins round its world—'

'Earth?'

'That's right. As it spins round Earth it drags the water in the seas, this way and that.'

'Tides! You told me.' Perhaps it wasn't a game . . .

'All those outer worlds are empty; too barren, too gaseous, too cold, hundreds of millions of kilometres from the sun. Its heat never reaches them. These two, Mercury and Venus, are too close. But this one, this little miracle, is in just the right place, not too hot, not too cold, two-thirds covered in water, and air all round it, just like this one.'

'Only thick.'

He laughed. 'Yes, thick air.'

'Is it like this one really? Do people live on it?'

'Oh yes,' he said, 'people live on it. The things that lived in the sea came out on land and breathed air, and grew legs – not all at once.' He saw that he was losing her. 'It took millions, billions of years. Some things stayed in the sea and became fish, and some things took to the air and flew.'

'Things lived in the air?' She looked up into the sky. 'You said it was *true*.'

'It is true, Dede. That's what I meant when I talked about flying. They travel in the air; they're called birds. I never imagined a world without birds until I saw it.'

Why did he keep insisting that this story was true when he was so clearly making it up? But it was a good story, she wanted more.

'Tell about the birds, how they lived in the air.'

'They are covered in feathers – think of leaves, little soft leaves. Think of a fish with arms and legs. Instead of scales it's covered in these leaves. When it wants to get off the ground it leaps into the air and spreads its arms – like this. They're called wings. It flaps its wings . . . and off it goes.' He tried to show her.

'Like swimming?'

'Yes, like swimming in the air. Some of them can't go very far, some stay up for months.'

'What's a month?'

'It's . . . oh, never mind. Four weeks. They make their homes in trees, under roofs, in cliffs.'

'Are they as big as people?'

'A few are, but that kind can't fly. Some are this big –' he spread his arms again – 'wing tip to wing tip, and some are tiny, like this, like my thumb, like your thumb, even. And they sing. When you wake up in the morning, you hear them singing.'

'Like you did, up and down?'

'No, not like me, not words. Very high and sweet, a kind of whistling.'

'And you flew here? You swam through the sky?'

'Not quite. For hundreds of years people watched birds and wished they could fly too, and tried, but they didn't know how. In the end they made machines, like boats with wings, and flew inside them, all around their world. And when they could fly around their world, in the sky, they looked beyond the sky, at the stars.'

'Did they want to go to the stars?'

'First of all they went to their moon, then they visited the planets, the other worlds that circled the sun.' He traced the orbits with his finger and drew a spiral in the sand that ran from pebble to pebble across the rings. 'But by this time their world was in trouble. They thought it would die.'

'How can a world die?'

'Oh, very easily, Dede, if you stop it breathing. First they cut down the trees . . . But anyway, they set out, beyond their solar system, to look for a new world to live on. It took a century, but in the end they found a star, a sun, and spinning round it was another little miracle – a planet, a world – like the one they lived on; not too close to the sun, not too distant, and it was fertile. There were fish in the seas, but nothing had come out yet to live on land except little creeping insects.'

'Or in the air? No birds?'

'No birds. They named it after one of their old goddesses—'

'What's a goddess?'

'I'll explain another time. They called it Demeter – the mother of all things growing.'

'That's my name almost.'

'Dede?'

'It's short for Demetria.'

'You must be called after Demeter then.'

'I don't know. Must I?'

'Well, it's a lovely thing to be named after your own planet.'

'What do you mean, my own planet?'

'Oh, Dede, Demetria, haven't you worked it out yet?' Crawling again he drew a line in the sand with his fingertip, from the pebble Earth to the pebble Demeter. 'This is your world, remember; this is Demeter. And because no one lived there they left their dying Earth and came to live here in the new world. They came with animals and seeds, across the universe, in a ship named the Ark, to start again. They were very careful about what they brought with them. No predators, no fast breeders, like rabbits. Even the rats didn't make it this time.'

'And did Earth die?'

'No, it didn't die. It recovered, got better; it became safe, a good place to live again. But by that time things on Demeter were not so good. People were beginning to quarrel and fight, just as they had done on Earth. They began to cut down the trees – that's where your logs come from, Dede. Whole forests destroyed to clear the land for oil-seed crops. They wanted to fly, on a planet where nothing had ever flown, and for that you need oil. On Earth they got it out of the ground, it's called petroleum, but there's no petroleum here. You've had no Carboniferous period.'

'What?'

'Another time. Anyway, some people grew afraid that the same thing would happen on Demeter as happened on Earth, so they called home for help. And a group of scientists – people who know how things work, say – got into one of those flying ships and travelled through space to try and help. But when they arrived, not everyone was pleased to see them.'

'Oh.' It had been shaping up so well, into a happy story, and then sad, and then just as it seemed that things would turn out well, those people flying to the rescue like fishermen putting out to sea to save a foundering boat, it all went flat again, and now it was going to end badly, like every other story. 'What happened then?'

'The ship came down in the wrong place. It was destroyed. Most of the people who came from Earth were killed and some of the men who had sent for them were arrested and sent to prison.'

'On the Low Island?' It was all becoming too real. He was not making up the Low Island.

'I don't think so, but I don't know. Isn't the Low Island for criminals, killers?'

'Bad people.'

'I wonder. But these weren't bad people and some of them were sent to another island where they couldn't get away and no one would talk to them. It's called exile.'

'The island is? Ex Isle?'

'No, not the island, the sending away. They couldn't even talk to each other much. Their letters were censored—'

'We've got a censor. I don't know what he does though.'

'I'll tell you some time. They had no other way of keeping in touch, the island had lost all its communications. It was very far from their homes. And one of them is so far from his home he can never go back.'

His eyes lingered on the far side of the patch of sand, on the solar system, then he raised his head and looked up at the peak. 'He was born at the foot of a mountain, Yr Wyddfa, and now he may die at the foot of this one, half the universe away.'

'What does it mean?' Demetria said.

'Mean?'

'Stories mean something, they're about what happens when you do the wrong thing, like the mermaid in the fisherman's net. I know!' Suddenly she got the point. 'The Earth people shouldn't have tried to fly. They didn't have those wing things so they should have stayed on the ground.'

He laughed; it was almost a howl. 'I suppose that's one way of looking at it. But, Dede, don't you understand, it isn't a story, it happened. There was no one living on land on this world until men came from Earth. And those poor devils who were sent into exile, they're called political prisoners. They didn't steal or kill, it was their ideas people didn't like. That's why they're here. You call them Politicals. Dede, they're real, they're us. I'm one of them.

'I told you, didn't I, how I must have done a terrible thing to be sent here. Well, that's the terrible thing I did. I left my home, my world, my children, their mother, to help people who asked for help.'

'It's not a story?' Demetria said. 'It's real?'

'It's real. On the mainland there are things you couldn't dream of even if I described them to you: forests thousands of kilometres across, rivers wider than the strait, fields full of flowers, trees as tall as the lighthouse, buildings as high as that cliff, all made of steel and glass, great roads and bridges and railways—'

His imagination was running away with him again. She would try to catch him out.

'Birds?'

'No, no birds, I wasn't lying. There are no birds living on this world.'

Give him one last chance. 'There aren't *really* birds anywhere, are there? You made them up.'

'What else do you think I made up?' he said sadly.

She hung her head. 'I don't know.'

'Do you think I'd lie to you?'

'Stories aren't lies. Well, they are if you pretend they're true and then hit people if they don't believe you.'

'Do you think I'd hit you? I never hit anyone . . . except . . .'

'Who did you hit?'

'When the guards came to arrest me I fought back, but there were three of us and twenty of them, with weapons. I didn't do much damage.'

'That bit's true then?'

'It's all true.'

'Except the birds.'

'Dede, you have to believe the birds. If men can't fly, how did they get here? How did they ever get off the Earth? How did they ever get off the ground? They'd never have thought of flying if they hadn't seen birds do it. They'd have known what an insane idea it was, to defy gravity—' He broke off. 'That's the trouble, isn't it? You do think it's an insane idea, because you've never seen it.' Suddenly he smiled and she realized how rarely he did smile, but then that was true of most people. He stood up and strode down to the water's edge, beckoning her to follow. 'Let's find a pebble, a nice flat one.'

'Like for hop-toad?'

'What's that – oh, that game you play, is it? You don't have toads here.'

'Of course we do. They're little polties.'

'Little what?'

'Polty are fish, but when they first hatch they come on land and hop about – you see them on the rocks, in spring, and here on the beach sometimes. And the little polties are called hop-toads. You must never kill a hop-toad or it won't grow up and lay eggs and one day there won't be any more polty.'

'That's something they learned on Earth the hard way,' he said. 'Anyway, yes, a nice flat round hop-toad pebble, lots of them, some for you, some for me.'

When they had a little cairn of hop-toad stones he took up a handful at random and gave her one. 'Now drop it.'

'Why?'

'Just drop it.' He let fall one of his and it clacked on the shingle. Demetria dropped hers. 'And what happened?'

'It fell.'

'Of course it did, that's gravity – no, never mind. Gravity's what makes things fall, stops us all floating off into space. Leave it at that for now.' He dropped another into the shallows and it vanished with a pleasing plop.

Demetria opened her hand and let all the pebbles go. 'This is silly. I know how things fall. Stones don't float.'

'But they can fly.' He picked up one of the hoptoad pebbles, crooking his index finger round it, stooped, drew back his arm and let it go. It sped low over the calm water, touched the surface with a little splash and rose again in a smooth arc, fell, rose. She counted. The fourth time it hit the water it did not rise again.

'How did you do that?'

'I'm out of practice.' He spun another stone. This one bounced five times before it vanished. 'Now do you believe me? Even stones can fly.'

'That's flying? Can I make them do that?'

'You mean, you never have? Does no one . . . ?' He showed her how to hold the stone, how to make it spin. They used up a lot of stones before she got the hang of it, but at last one of hers bounced; once, twice, before it sank.

'That's the idea, try again, keep it low. You'll be beating me soon.'

'Is this a game then?'

'No, it's advanced physics.' She ignored that, she could read his voice now. 'Of course it's a game – we call it Ducks and Drakes. But look, the stone is moving so fast when it hits the water it has enough energy to rise up again, but each time it's lost a little of that energy, each time it flies a shorter distance and

113

in the end, all the energy is used up and it sinks. But if it had wings now, it could keep going, up and up.'

'Is that how birds fly, bouncing on water? Oh, look – *five* times.'

'No, but they spring from the ground . . . and from water, now that you mention it, and the air flows over their wings and under them. I wish I could show you. If I had some paper I could make a plane, but they wouldn't sell me any.'

'And there's people coming,' Demetria said, pointing towards the rocks at the harbour end of the beach. 'Market's over.'

'Better for you that we go then,' Ianto Morgan said. He spun one last stone – ten splashes – and turned away. 'No, I'll go, you stay here and see if Tycho brings you anything.' He started to walk up the beach, then looked round, suddenly.

'I know! I'll show you what flying is, Dede. I'll make you a kite.'

10

What was a kite?

She wished that there was someone she could ask, but she dared not. Knitting in the classroom beside Stephane, free to talk now that she had mastered heels and toes, she longed to say, casually, 'Do you know what a kite is?' 'Have you ever heard of something called a kite?' 'It would be nice to have a kite, wouldn't it?' But then Stephane almost certainly would not know, would ask where she had heard the word. She might carry it away with her and try it on someone else and then reveal that she had heard it from Demetria who could never, ever tell where she had got it from.

And if Ianto Morgan kept his word and made one for her, she would know soon enough. She probably would not see him again until Senday when everyone else was out of the way. She did not know where he went during the week while she was in school, although wherever it was it could not be far. She never saw him on the quayside again, making a conspiracy. He knew better now.

The days were lengthening. The sun was up now before she went to school and set well after she returned so she did not see him even on his way to report to the barracks. But if he was out of sight, he was never out of mind. She could not look at the stars now without thinking of the patterns on the sand, his strange story of the man who travelled through the sky, among the stars, so far that he could never go home again to his planet and his children and the mother of his children – the family that he didn't hit. The mother of his children . . . he didn't call her his wife. How could that be?

Next Senday she must ask him which of the stars was his, which was the sun and its planet Earth, with its enormous moon that hung in the sky like another white world and gave enough light for people to see their way at night. He had said that sometimes it was so bright that you could not see the stars. Did he look at his star and think of his children?

And did they, on their Earth, look into the night sky, searching for this sun, and think of him?

Did anyone else know what she knew, that this world was not just called The World – that it had a name, like hers: Demeter. She wanted to ask about that too. Only Mam would know, and she had to be asked carefully.

'Mam, why am I called Demetria?'

Mam stared at her as if she could not understand why she would ask.

'It's your name.'

She knew she was risking a slap. 'Yes, but why?'

'It was your father's idea. Demetrius if you were a boy. He wanted Demetrius for Bevis, but I wasn't having it. Still, when you came along, him being dead, it was the least I could do.'

Now she knew something about her father – the only thing. He had wanted her to have a lovely name. So that was something else to cherish as a comforting secret. *It's a lovely thing to be named after your own planet*, Ianto Morgan had said.

How much of his story had been untrue, and if it was untrue, why was he so desperate for her to believe it? All that about huge buildings and great long roads and bridges on the mainland. They had a bridge further up the hillside, over the ravine where the Blackwater came down, trickling in summer, gushing in the autumn rains or with meltwater in spring, but the bridge was only as wide as the path it carried, and the stream was no wider than a street. When it reached the harbour it was channelled into a culvert that ran under the quayside. That was a kind of bridge too. Why would anyone need a *big* bridge? What would cross it, what would it cross? And those great tall buildings, higher than the cliff, all glass and steel, what would you put in a building that high? She tried to picture it but could only imagine the barracks, the tallest building on the quayside, five times, ten times higher, higher than the lighthouse, with its steep metal roof still perched on top. There was nothing amazing about that; it looked very silly.

They had not arranged to meet anywhere, at any time, which turned out to be just as well. On Senday morning Mam stood outside the kitchen door, tested the air and called to Bevis.

'You can get the root garden turned over today. If this weather holds we can plant in a week or two.'

'Mam, there's still pillocks—'

'There's plenty of others to gather pillocks. Don't forget to clean the spade when you've done.'

'What about her?' Bevis scowled at Demetria.

'She'll fetch the shopping as usual.'

Washing up, after Mam had gone to market, Demetria looked out of the window. The root garden was at the far end, between the gate and the shed, where Ianto Morgan's tray was out on the step, waiting to be fetched. Bevis was already digging. The top of the garden, nearer to the house and more sheltered, was where they grew pulses, plants that writhed their way up frames of twigs and canes, putting out sweet-scented blossoms in early summer. She liked to watch the pea-beetles at work among them, darting into the flowers and lumbering out again, furred with pollen. Some people, she knew, kept a little patch especially for growing flowers, but Mam didn't. You could not eat flowers.

She was ready to empty the basin of washing-up water, but the tray, with its bowl and mug, still sat on the step of the shed. Bevis was not going to bring it in. She dried her hands and went down the path to fetch it.

'Where do you think you're going?' Bevis said as she went by.

'For the tray – I want to wash the dishes.'

'Wait till I bring it in.'

'The water's still hot, can you bring it in now?'

'When I'm ready.'

'I can't go shopping till I've finished.'

'You'll have to wait then.'

He had done something like this so often before, spoiling her day with orders of his own invention, cuffing her if she argued. But she wanted to get out of the house, down to the quayside. It was worth risking a cuff.

And perhaps Ianto Morgan was still in the shed. No, it was ages since the bell had rung, but he might have come back. He might come out and *defend* her. He could not stop Bevis hitting her but he might bestow a few of those hard words on him: thug, bully, brat. She walked past her brother to the shed, and picked up the tray.

'I told you to leave it.' Bevis sounded incredulous.

She took no notice, walked steadily back to the

house, tensed all the way for the blow to fall. He would never let her get away with it. But he must have been so amazed by her defiance that he almost left it too late. She was at the door before the clod of stone-hard soil hit her between the shoulders, the impact shooting the bowl and mug off the tray and bowling them across the kitchen floor.

She managed not to look round. Ianto Morgan could not be in the shed or he would have come out, but it hardly mattered. She had disobeyed Bevis and now she had the confidence to close the kitchen door still without looking round, as though he had not thrown the missile and it had not struck her; or it had been such a feeble effort that it really was not worth bothering about. She knew now, there was no need to be hit. She knew a man who said he didn't hit his children. For some reason it never occurred to her to wonder if he might be lying about that too. She was sure that if he had a sister he had never hit her either. She had seen his anger, and how he controlled it. No matter what she said to him, he was never angry with her.

This week there had been no sign of Ianto Morgan at the shops. She had not seen him since last Senday when he had shown her how to play duxendrakes, how to make stones fly; since he had told her the story she could not believe and then walked quickly away so that she might not get into trouble for talking to him.

120

Had he made her a kite, whatever that was? If he had said he would, then he would do it, but what was it, what would he make it of? He had nothing except for what he could buy and he couldn't have much money, wherever it came from. If he had money, he'd be living in a house and drinking in the tavern.

She ran into Stephane outside the general store.

'Let's go and look at the grave,' Stephane said. Demetria did not want to look at the grave, she wanted to be on the beach, just in case, where he would see her even if they could not talk.

'All right, but let's go to the beach afterwards.' If only she could teach Stephane how to play duxendrakes without Stephane wanting to know where Demetria had picked up such an odd game.

The grave was almost empty. Their bottle had gone, she was pleased to see, and all the shoes. The only things left were small heavy objects – the odd coin, a plate, a bone comb. But she could tell Mam that Tycho had taken their bottle back. That might please her.

It was very windy today. People who wanted to talk sheltered against the harbour wall; the men went into the tavern. Only a few children had ventured over the rocks to the beach. Demetria looked eagerly along the crescent of sand where the white waves ramped and crashed, flinging the spray high. You couldn't play duxendrakes on those breakers. Anyway, what was a duxendrake? Was it like a garden rake? Why would you throw it? She ought to have asked him. She had added this latest new word to all the others: goddess, gravity, electricity, turbine, generator, petroleum. When they had time he would tell her.

Ianto Morgan was not there and the patch of sand where he had drawn his star systems was underwater now. Was he up at the shed? Or perhaps he was on the path, looking down, hoping to see her. No, the path was empty.

Debris littered the beach: broken boxes, torn nets, floats, even dead fish. Stephane gathered up shards of wood and bound them with twine that she had disentangled from a net. You could never pass up the chance of kindling – it saved splitting logs. Then she went back to town and her home near the Blackwater bridge; it was too cold to loiter on the sand. They could have played hop-toad, but it was impossible to jump far in the fierce wind.

Demetria started for home, up the path. She had gathered no kindling; she still had the heavy shopping basket to haul. Before she had climbed more than a few metres, she heard the voice.

'Dede.' And there he was, by a wall, out of the wind, out of sight from the beach. She looked at once for the kite, but he was empty-handed.

Perhaps it was something very small, in his pocket . . .

'Did you make my kite?'

'I tried, but look, you're going to have to help. Can you sew as well as knit?'

'Of course.'

'Put down your basket, I'll give you a hand with it later.' Out of his coat he drew a flat fold of red cloth, the kind used for making summer shirts and trousers, thin and light.

'Where did you get that?'

'I bought it, in the store. And I bought needles and thread. There's me thinking I'm a superman, but I'm no good at it. I broke my thumb when – a while back – and it won't bend right for holding a needle. I can throw stones but I can't sew. Can you put a hem round that for us?'

'It's a funny shape,' Demetria said as he shook it out.

'It's the shape it needs to be. Here's the needle and thread – they'd only sell me the one, don't break it for god's sake – and five metres of thread. Rationing, apparently, for Politicals. Perhaps they think that if they let us have too much we'll plait ropes and hang ourselves.'

'Didn't they want to know why it was this shape?'

'I didn't buy it this shape,' he said. 'I'm not stupid, not any more. I said I wanted to patch a shirt. They sold me a metre and I cut it out myself. I'm allowed to use a razor now.'

'You don't cut cloth with a razor,' Demetria said.

'You've got scissors? You can trim it a bit maybe.

123

I'm sorry, I didn't think ahead. I wanted to have it ready for you – this would be such a day for it.'

'Why?'

'Kites need wind. Now, when you sew the hem, you must make a little pocket at each corner. Can you do that?'

'Why does it need pockets?'

'You'll see. Only little ones, mind. Not quite big enough to fit your smallest finger.'

She looked at the frayed, gnawed edges of the cloth and knew how disappointed he must be at the mess he had made.

The midday hooter had only recently sounded.

'Mam won't be back yet. I'll take this home and trim it up with her scissors. Mine are too small, they're only for cutting yarn.' She hadn't the heart to tell him that she had her own needles and thread too, in the knitting bag. 'Then I'll come back here and sew it with you.'

'You can't sew out of doors, you'll freeze. Do it at home.'

'I can't,' she said, and he knew why.

'I'll help you with the basket.'

'No, I can manage. Stay here. I won't be long.'

Bevis was still digging. Demetria could hear the spadework from the street. She entered the house by the front door and rapidly unpacked the shopping. Then she went to the sewing chest, took out the long shears and sliced off the ragged edges from the

124

strange shape with its odd angles, taking care to gather up any telltale rags and threads. Then she left, closing the front door silently behind her, and raced down the street. Bevis, in the garden, never knew that she had been there.

'I couldn't even thread the needle for you,' he said. 'How will you sew with cold hands?' He looked at the reddened fingers poking out of her mittens.

'We've always got cold hands,' Demetria said. 'Everyone says, if we keep knitting our hands will get warm, but they don't.'

'Why don't you wear gloves?'

'We couldn't knit in gloves! We're out of the wind here, it's all right. Anyway, the weather's getting warmer. It'll be spring soon.'

'If you say so.' He watched admiringly as the needle slipped in and out of the fabric. She rolled the hem one-handed with her left thumb as it approached.

'Don't forget the pockets!'

'What's going in the pockets? Stones? Will you make stones fly with this?'

'God, no. Look.' Lying in the grass were two thin lengths of wood, one shorter than the other. He picked up the longer one, which was about the length of his arm from wrist to shoulder, held it between his fingertips and pressed until it curved into an arc.

'That won't be good for anything, it'll break.'

'Not the way I'll use it. I've been down to the beach every day, looking for something like these. Tycho brought them – that means he approves, doesn't it, because he sent this too. It's taken me two days to unravel it.' Out of his pocket he drew a short stub of wood and round it were wrapped metres of fishing line.

'All tangled up with the net, it was. I'd tried to buy some at the chandler's. That gave them a good laugh – a Political going fishing.'

'Are you going fishing?'

He sighed. 'No, Dede, I'm going to fly a kite.'

While she finished the final pocket, backstitched and snipped the thread, he was binding the two sticks crosswise. 'Lay the cloth out flat now.' He fitted the ends of the sticks carefully into the mysterious pockets and suddenly the limp cloth became taut.

'It's like a sail on a boat!'

'So it is. You know about sails, how the wind drives the boat. You've seen washing on a line, the way the wind fills it. You know what wind can do. Does a sheet or a dishtowel never blow loose and go flying? What about leaves in autumn?'

'That's not flying. They don't weigh anything. They come down. You said flying meant staying up.'

'But it's all about using air, isn't it? Wind is only air moving.'

'Is it?'

Now he was making a web with his fishing line,

attaching the crossed sticks to the long length on its reel that Tycho had sent him. Then he brought out of his pocket a handful of rags, white and blue, and bits of the red cloth.

'I could have cut those properly,' Demetria said.

'They don't need to be neat. These are for the tail. It must have a tail for balance.'

'Like a fish?'

'Like a bird.'

She saw that there was a loose end of line. He began knotting the rags to it.

'Let's make a pattern – two red . . . one white . . . one blue . . . one red . . . two white . . . one blue . . . one red –'

'Where did the other bits come from?'

'– one white . . . two blue . . . and a red one to finish it off. My shirts.'

He had only two shirts, she knew that from the laundry that Mam did, hung out in the garden on the long line. His few things were kept separate, at the far end of the line; *exiled*. The white shirt he had worn when he arrived, another he had bought since. He had cut off bits of his shirts to make a tail for her kite.

'You haven't got much money, have you?'

'Not a lot.'

'Where does it come from? Did they send it from – from Earth?'

He was just knotting the final red rag and looked up, half-smiling. 'You're trying to catch me out again,

127

aren't you? Now look, you must go home for your dinner. The second hooter's just gone; those poor devils over there will have finished their slop. No day off for them. Are you free this afternoon?'

'Free?'

'Have you got any work to do?'

There were always stockings to be darned, but if she went home now she could eat and be out again before Mam returned from market. She would have to be quick; there were already people on the beach.

'No.'

'Then come back straight after and we'll walk up the hill and fly the kite. It's best to be in a high place. And as we go I'll tell you where my money comes from.'

She started to leave, then a thought struck her. He'd forgotten something, or hadn't thought of it. Had she caught him out this time?

'Shall I bring some oil?'

'Whatever for?'

'The kite. You said people needed oil to fly.'

For some reason this made him smile again. 'People do, for the machines they fly in. All the kite will need is air.'

11

They did not have to walk very far in the fields before the land dipped and even the highest houses in the town were out of sight.

'Have you ever been up here before?' Ianto Morgan was looking ahead at the steep slope up to the top of the cliff.

'No.'

'Never out of the town?'

'No.'

'So you don't know what else is on this island of yours?'

'Sheep. People live up on the hills with the sheep.'

'That's not all, surely.'

'How would you know?' Aha! Got him. 'Is *that* where you come from, up the mountain?'

'Dear god, I told you where . . . I've seen maps of this island.'

'Maps are of the sea.'

'There are maps of all this world, Dede, of the oceans and the mainlands and the islands. When people first came here they landed on the other side of Demeter, on the mainland they called Baltica. This whole planet was mapped and named before anyone ever set foot on it. The other mainlands are Laurentia and Gondwana. The one you call *the* mainland is Laurentia. You didn't know that, did you?'

'You didn't know our drifts are called Tycho and Kepler.'

'I'm not an oceanographer,' he muttered, sounding almost irritable, then he grinned, more at himself than at her. 'Which I will explain another time. And what your mainlands are named after and why. We call them continents at home. From the start the ships from Earth touched down on Baltica; that's where our ship was headed. It has the facilities. But there was a technical fault, we had to make landfall too soon and came down over Laurentia. That's where we were needed – but not where we were wanted. That is, the people want us, the planet needs us, but not the Government of Laurentia.

'Those people who asked us to come, you know them, Dede. They're the Politicals, and they still want us . . . want me. I may be the only one left.

'But our friends in Baltica keep in touch. They send money and letters to political prisoners so that we know we aren't forgotten. That's what keeps us hoping, keeps us sane. And the Government of Laurentia dare not do away with us because of them, so they send us to these islands – there are others like this – while they work out what to do. Though I doubt there are any others *quite* like this one,' he added under his breath.

'This isn't a big world. To keep the air clean the people who first settled here travelled by sea. They still do, but anyone who had air supremacy . . .'

The incline was growing steeper and the winter grass was lumpy underfoot. Ianto Morgan was slowing down, the thin air sighing in his chest. He stopped and bent over, hands braced on knees, apparently examining the small buds that were beginning to show in the shelter of the tussocks.

'What are they called?'

'I don't know. They're flowers . . . will be.'

'I can see that.'

'When it's summer they all come out at once. Everything looks yellow, the hills, the fields.'

'But no bees or butterflies.'

'What are they?'

'Something else that can fly. Insects that carry pollen from flower to flower.'

'We have beetles to do that. They jump, like hoptoads. Like – like duxendrakes.'

'Ah well, when birds jump, they stay up. On Earth beetles can fly too.'

'Does everything that flies begin with a B?'

'Birds, bees, butterflies . . . bats. Ballistic

missiles . . . but not kites. Come on, save your breath now, or rather I'll save mine. You've got the lungs for this atmosphere. Let's concentrate on getting to the top.' He straightened up and started walking again.

She looked behind her from time to time as they climbed. She had never been this far, this high. The folds of the fields lay below them, then the ridge over which they had walked, and now the town was in sight again. She could not believe how small it was, the rooftops with their smoking chimneys, clustering along the sides of the Blackwater, down to the harbour and the rocks. The mole was no more than an eyebrow in the sea. The beach was out of sight and only the lantern of the lighthouse was visible above a shoulder of the mountain.

As they came up on to the clifftop the wind tore about them. Strangely, it was less violent up here, but much colder. She stood looking all around while he did the hands-on-knees thing again, recovering his breath. Back the way they had come lay the town. Had she not known what it was she would have thought the rooftops were haphazard slabs of rock where the stream had cut its way down to the harbour. It looked like a cascade of stones, and for the first time she saw why it was built there, in the little bay scooped out by Tycho, the one place where you could get on and off the island. And now she saw how the Blackwater had got its name, tumbling over and through the slash in the black rock of the mountain.

Ahead the land continued to rise and fall, but each time rising higher than before, then gathering itself into a green surge up to the peak, still white-capped with snow as though it really were a frozen wave. And the island went on and on. She could not see the edge.

On the lower slopes were little grey-white dots like outcrops of snow. But –

'Look! They're moving.'

'They're sheep,' Ianto Morgan said. 'Dear child, you and your knitting, have you never seen a sheep?'

'Knitting? Oh, the wool. I've seen pictures.'

'Well, there's the real thing. So they let them over-winter on the hills here, and they'll lamb in spring, the old way.'

'Can you hear that? Are they singing?'

He stood listening to the faint, far-off voices, seemingly trying not to laugh. 'Not precisely,' he said at last. 'My god, the song of the sheep. What a thought. Does no one from the town come up here?'

'I don't know. The shepherds bring the wool down in summer. It isn't on the sheep though.'

'Where do the shepherds live?'

'I don't know.'

'There used to be an observatory up here once,' he said, 'out on the plateau, I suppose.'

'What's an observatory?'

'A place to study the stars,' he said. 'Telescopes.'

'To look through?'

'Some were, but there was a radio telescope too. It was a whole set of dishes. No, not like the porridge bowls – tens of metres across. That was why people first came here, to this island, to build and man the observatory. It would have been on the far side of the peak. That was one of the first things to go.'

She could not follow his description. A telescope was a long tube with glass discs at each end. Dishes? Enormous dishes? 'Are we going to fly the kite?'

'Why else did we come? Now, the wind's coming off the sea, but we must be very careful to stay away from the edge of the cliff. I'd be sorry to go over in the excitement.'

'Is it exciting?'

'I hope so. But let's just look, first, so you'll remember how high up we are. It'll be a long drop.'

The grassy slope ended sharply, as though someone had brought down a heavy knife and sheared the land away with a single sweep.

'Don't go any closer in this wind,' he said when they were about five metres away. 'It could have you off your feet. But look at the sea, how far down it is. Can you swim?'

'Of course not. Girls can't swim. Boys have to learn – because of going on the boats.'

'And you're not allowed to?'

'No, we'd sink. We aren't made right, women aren't.'

'For crying out loud!' he shouted. 'What utter

bloody rubbish. Of course you can swim. Who says you can't?'

'It's true.'

'It's *not* true. Remember that, Dede. It's a lie. Not *made* right? You're perfect. If you can float, you can swim. Anyone can swim. Even I can.'

'Nobody *wants* to swim,' she said, 'except – except – the Low Islanders.'

As she said it she looked. The Low Island was no longer a hazy presence on the horizon, it was visible land, on her side of the skyline; she could see buildings.

'When the Banshee sounds, someone's swimming.'

'Oh yes. That's when they turn off the lighthouse, isn't it? In case he might see where he was going.'

The lighthouse was in sight again, beyond the town, a blunt fingertip raised above the rocks as if testing the wind.

'Oh look, there's a whale!'

'*What?* You don't have whales in these oceans.'

'We do. The log, there, all on its own, that's a whale. The little ones are dolphins. I wonder if it will come to land.'

'Well, you know where it will go if it doesn't, don't you?'

'No. Do you?'

'On round the island, through the strait – until it reaches Baltica. Sooner or later everything that leaves Laurentia reaches Baltica and Gondwana. And the other way about; what goes around comes around. Good old Tycho. At least, that's what ought to happen. I wonder, do the logs touch shore at the Low Island ever?'

'I don't know.'

'Do you know why they're called whales and dolphins?'

'They just are.'

'What's the biggest fish in your sea?'

'The orn. It's, oh –' she stretched her arms – 'longer than that.'

'Not so very long then. In the seas on Earth there are creatures, not fish, bigger than your fishing boats – thirty metres long, some of them longer. The big ones are whales, the little ones are dolphins, and we nearly lost them all. But just in time we stopped killing them.'

'Why did you kill them?'

'Because they were there,' he said.

Creatures as big as boats? There he went again with his crazy tales. Time to put that craziness to the test. 'Let's fly the kite.'

'Let's hope it works,' he muttered. To carry the kite he had removed the sticks and rolled the cloth round them. He reassembled it and said, 'Now, hold it in both hands, hold it up above your head, firmly, mind, or the wind will take it before you're ready. When I say run, go that way, down-wind of me.'

'What are you going to do?'

'I've got the string,' he said, holding up the reel of fishing line. 'Now, run. And when you feel the kite's ready to go, let it.'

'How will I know?'

'You'll know.'

She set off across the slope, and at once the wind caught the kite, but she hung on until the tugging became too strong and it was blowing her along as if she were a boat under sail. It rose from her hands, the tail flicked her face, and then the kite was above her. She could not see the fishing line, the kite seemed to be up there on its own, not blown helplessly like escaped laundry but bucking and swooping, riding the air as boats rode the drifts. And its every move was controlled, she saw now, by Ianto Morgan on the other end of the line, his arm rising and falling, beckoning, playing the invisible string.

The kite went up and up, its tail streaming. She ran back to him. 'How far will it go?'

'As far as the line will let it. I can reel it in any time. Do you want to hold it? Just do what I do, play it like a fish, pull against its tugging, gently, gently, gently . . .'

She took the stub of wood and immediately felt the kite strain like a living thing at the end of its leash.

'All right?' Ianto Morgan said. 'Do you see? Do you feel it? That's flying.'

Tycho had been generous, giving him so much line. Little by little she paid it out and the kite went on and on, higher, higher than the peak it seemed, swerving, diving, climbing, the bright tail rippling gallantly behind it.

Then it began to fall and she felt the line slacken in spite of her tugging.

'Oh no! It's coming down. What can I do?'

She let her arm drop. Ianto Morgan ran to meet her, took the reel and began to jog backwards, shortening the line until the kite recovered and soared again.

'Should we give it a rest?'

She did not notice that he could hardly speak. 'No, no. Not yet. Let it fly. Let it fly!' She danced and spun across the grass, head tipped back, while he stood against the sky, coat flapping, hair everywhere, gasping and laughing at her, and the kite kept climbing, climbing –

It seemed to falter and at the same moment a shot cracked nearby, rolling round and round the echoing land, up to the peak and down again. She stopped. He was staring upwards. A second shot hit the wooden sticks, the kite collapsed, a rag at the end of its tether, and began to fall, fluttering in the wind.

There were voices. Over the edge of the slope heads appeared – people, soldiers; shouting, running. Demetria turned, skidded, fell and stayed down. Some terrible thing had happened, the soldiers were running into battle, the enemy must be up ahead, out there where the sheep were. She and Ianto Morgan were in the way. Suppose the enemy shot back? Perhaps it was they who had fired first – hit the kite – the kite –

The soldiers were closing in on Ianto Morgan. He seemed at last to understand what was happening and began to run. Demetria screamed, 'Not that way! The cliff! The cliff!', but he kept going until another shot was fired. She did not see where it hit him, perhaps it did not, but he stumbled, fell to his knees, staggered half-upright again and tried to run on, but two of the soldiers had caught up with him now, one of them swinging his weapon by the barrel like a club.

And two more were coming for her.

She crouched on the grass, arms wrapped round her head, making herself as small as possible, waiting for the blow that would smash down on her too. But there was only a voice – not even an angry voice – gruff but gentle.

'It's all right. No one's going to hurt you.'

He kept on saying it. 'No one's going to hurt you. You're safe now. No one's going to hurt you. It's all right.'

When at last she looked up the two men had laid down their weapons and were kneeling in front of her, open-handed, to show that they really meant her no harm. But they were blocking her view. She did not see what had happened to Ianto Morgan.

Part Three

Part Three

12

The sergeant carried her down because her legs would not move. Over his shoulder she saw another soldier carrying the remains of the kite, the tail carefully draped between his hands as though it were something very important.

She was so tired, her eyes kept closing, but every time she opened them, there was the kite, coming down the hillside behind her. Had they rescued it or captured it? What had happened to Ianto Morgan?

Now they were crossing the beach; there was the place where he had drawn his star systems, where they had played duxendrakes.

Now they were going up the rocky steps, on to the quay. People were standing in groups, silent, staring. No one even raised an arm to point. There was no sound but the tramp of the soldiers' boots over the stones. She closed her eyes again before she saw someone she knew. If her face were hidden they might not know it was her.

She had never been into the barracks before, not even into the yard. When it had been derelict boards had barred the doors and windows, and there had been no yard until the wall had gone up round it. The crash of boots echoed in the corridor. The only thing she noticed was how warm it was inside. They were in a big room with pipes crossing the ceiling, then a small room. The sergeant sat her down in a chair and someone put a rug round her shoulders, saying, 'She's shivering,' and someone else said, 'Shock.' They gave her a mug of something hot, but her hands were too weak to hold it and when another hand lifted it gently to her mouth it chattered against her teeth. Any moment now they would start hitting her.

When she raised her eyes at last she expected to see a circle of men with weapons, but there was only a high window with glass that she could not see through, and a big desk like the Master had in his office at school. The sergeant was sitting behind it. Another man, who had only one stripe on his sleeve, sat astride a chair in the corner, his arms folded across the back.

'Demetria, isn't it?' the sergeant said. 'Demetria Joyce.'

He spoke quietly, with the accent that marked him as a mainlander. She had expected him to shout, because clearly she and Ianto Morgan had done something wrong, dreadfully wrong. He would shout, then he would hit her, or someone else would. She looked round, but there was no one behind her. The corporal did not move from his chair.

'You needn't be afraid,' the sergeant said. 'I meant it, no one will hurt you. You didn't do anything wrong.'

'She'd have been told to stay away from him,' the corporal said suddenly, unexpectedly. 'Isn't that right?' He turned to face her. 'Your mother told you not to talk to him?' He swung back to the sergeant. 'She disobeyed her mother. Perhaps it's a little early to promise that no one will hurt her. Have you seen the brother?'

They knew who she was. They knew Mam and Bevis.

'We have to ask you some questions,' the sergeant said, 'about your friend Ianto.'

Her friend? Had they been friends? She had never thought of him like that. She had never even called him Ianto.

Finally she managed to speak, although there was no sound in her voice, only gritty breath. Her tongue felt fat and heavy, filling her mouth, the words dribbled out like water. She could not swallow. 'Where is he?'

'He's not here any more, Demetria. He's had to go away.'

'He's dead!' He fell over the cliff, that's why they hadn't let her see . . .

'No, no, he's not dead. But people like him, your guests, they're only allowed to live on your island as long as they behave themselves. You know that.'

'Yes. He told me.'

They were both alert now.

'What did he tell you, Demetria?'

Was it a trap? 'He said he must have done something very terrible to be sent here.'

'Did he, now? And did he tell you what that terrible thing was?'

Repeating what he had said couldn't do any harm. They were his guards. They must know.

'He said he came from another world because he'd been asked for help.'

'Another *world*?'

'A planet. With a big moon that dragged the sea up mountains.' She knew she was getting it wrong, but her jaw was juddering, her head ached, she ached all over. 'And there were things like fish with legs, covered in leaves.'

The two men looked at each other.

'Fish covered in leaves,' the sergeant said encouragingly.

'That went up in the air – *birds*.' It all became clear again. 'That's why we made the kite.'

'A kite?'

'You shot it down. That was the kite. He wanted to show me what flying was.'

'He called it a kite, did he? How did he make it?'

'I sewed it, he'd hurt his thumb. He put it together and made the tail.'

'Ah, yes – the tail. And what was the tail for?'

'To – to *balance* it. Birds have tails.'

'And why did you take it up on to the cliffs?'

'For the wind – it needed wind to fly. And so I wouldn't get into trouble. If anyone had seen us on the beach—'

'I don't think he was very worried about your getting into trouble, Demetria, or he wouldn't have befriended you in the first place. He knew it was wrong. That kite, as you call it, was no game. He used you as an excuse to fly it, and he used you to make it.' His voice became stern. He reached under the desk and held something up at arm's length. It was the kite, broken and draggled, the muddied rags of the tail drooping from the fishing line. It looked dead. It *was* dead, shot through the heart, torn and bleeding. 'Tell me about this tail. Why is it all different colours?'

'It was all he had, bits of the cloth he bought and . . . he cut the rest from his shirts.'

'Do you really think he'd cut up his clothes just to make a toy for you?' He did not wait for an answer. 'Why are the colours arranged like this – red, red; white, blue, red; white, white; blue, red, white; blue, blue; red?'

'He said, "Let's make a pattern."'

'It wasn't a pattern. This is a code, a signal. He was trying to get round the censor, do you understand?'

'I don't know what the censor does.'

'He goes through the priso— through the *guests'* mail and cuts out anything they shouldn't know and shouldn't be telling. Morgan was signalling with this – this kite – to someone who knew what that code means. That's why he put your life at risk, dragging you up to the cliff in this wind. He wanted the message to be seen.'

'He didn't. Didn't put my life at risk. He didn't drag me. He told me to be careful.'

'Telling's easy. Did he threaten you? Did he make you go up there?'

'No. He never made me do anything. We played games.'

The corporal coughed, meaningly. The sergeant glanced at him and looked back at Demetria. He seemed embarrassed.

'What games?'

'It was a game with stones, throwing them. Duxendrakes.'

'Did he ever touch you?'

'Touch me?'

'Anywhere?'

'No, never . . . only . . .'

'Only?' The sergeant was frowning.

'When he gave me the kite string to hold. He put it in my hand.'

'That's all?' The corporal was looking out of the window that you couldn't see through.

'He told me stories.'

'He told you lies.'

'No, they *weren't* lies.' Weren't they? 'He told me about his children.'

'Oh, he's got children now, has he?' the corporal said. 'What about his sweet old mother?'

'Not *his* mother, his children's mother. He said he'd never see them again.'

'Since they don't exist, I don't suppose he will,' the corporal said. 'What about his friends?'

'I don't think he had any friends. Only me.'

The sergeant sighed. 'There's no need to cry for him.' She had not known that she was crying. 'He used you. He pretended to be your friend, but he wasn't. He was an evil man and you won't have to see him again. There'll be no more lies about flying fish and making patterns—'

The question she had been struggling to shape was on her tongue at last. 'Who was the signal for?'

'That's what we have to find out,' the corporal said. 'No need for you to bother your head about it. Forget him and his lies. You're a nice girl, Demetria. Are you a good girl? You do as your mother says, in future, and stay away from the guests. They're not here for fun. It's a shame you have to put up with them, but that's the way of it. You won't make this mistake again, will you?'

He nodded to the sergeant. 'Find someone to take her home.'

'I don't need taking home,' Demetria said.

The sergeant sighed again. 'I think you do.'

It was one of the ordinary guards who escorted her, and as they stepped out of the door she was glad to feel his big heavy presence beside her. Her legs were still weak and they might have given way altogether when she saw the silent crowds still gathered on the quayside, all gazing towards the barracks, towards its door, towards her. They were no longer silent. A low muttering hung around them – not the conversation of market days – although, she realized with a start, it was still market day – but a puzzled, angry buzz. And something was going on in the background behind them, much rushing about and shouting, but it all seemed very muffled and distant like the soldier's voice or the sound she had heard as they walked along the corridor which she hadn't been able to identify, but it had sounded like a scream. It had sounded like a man screaming, but it couldn't be that. Why would a man scream . . . ?

The soldier took her hand. 'Brave girl,' he said quietly. 'Keep walking.' They left the yard, crossed the mole, and headed towards the upper end of the quayside where her street began. Behind them she heard the voice of the corporal addressing the crowd.

'There's nothing more to concern yourselves about. The matter's being dealt with, you have nothing to fear. Go home now.'

Normally the guards did not speak to the islanders unless it were necessary – certainly never gave them orders. And why was the corporal so much more in charge than the sergeant? But that part of it was over now, for her. They were walking up the street, away from the harbour, and with every turn of the road, with every step they took, home was drawing closer. That part had not even begun yet.

'Do we knock at the door?' her soldier said, 'or go in by the side gate?'

'Side gate,' Demetria whispered. It was standing open. Were Mam and Bevis down on the quayside among the crowd? As they went in she saw that the whole of the root garden had been dug over. Was it only this morning that Mam had told Bevis to go out and do it? So much had happened in the one short day. The sun was setting now.

She saw too that the door of Ianto Morgan's shed was open. Could he have come back?

Something lay across the step, long and dark. A person? A body?

It was a blanket from the bed. Then, as if one thing after another were gradually coming into focus, she saw the bed, upended, overturned on the path, with the mattress and pillow flung aside. The bucket, the basin, the tripod were strewn across the turned earth, and the chair . . . it was broken . . .

They were at the kitchen door.

There was a soldier in the kitchen. Mam and Bevis were sitting at the table and no one was speaking. They did not look up.

'Well, here she is,' the soldier said. 'Home safe and sound.'

'Absolutely safe and sound,' Demetria's soldier said. The two of them sounded so cheerful, as if nothing much had happened. 'You needn't worry, Mother Joyce,' the other soldier said cosily to Mam. 'She came to no harm at all. Badly frightened by the looks of it, but not harmed.'

How did he know?

When they had gone, apologizing for any inconvenience, no one moved. Mam and Bevis sat at the table. Demetria stood where her soldier had left her, in the middle of the kitchen floor. She felt sick, as if Bevis were already punching her in the stomach. Her mouth was full of sour spit. The silence went on and on; the room was growing darker by the second as the sun sank. When Bevis stood up and struck her across the face, so hard that she staggered against the wall, it was almost a relief. The awful stillness was broken.

Mam said, 'They searched the house.'

'They came up here and searched the shed. They

152

took everything that vermin had in there,' Bevis said. His hand swept round again. 'And then they came in here and looked in everything, every room, every cupboard, every drawer, every chest. That's your doing, you dirty little toad, creeping about with *him*, lying, sneaking. He's a spy, he's a traitor and you've been helping him.'

'How shall we face people now?' Mam said in a drab monotone. She still had not looked Demetria in the eye. 'You know what they'll call us – collaborators.'

'He's a criminal – they're all criminals. He's a thief, he's a liar, and you helped him. He was signalling to the enemy and you *helped* him—'

Demetria found her voice. 'What enemy?'

'Shut up!' Another swipe. 'They sent him here because he was too disgusting to have at home. They *paid* us to have him here and they'll never send us another one, because of *you*.' As she recalled, vaguely, they had never wanted a Political in the first place. Surely they couldn't be angry about the money?

'Where have they sent him?'

'It's none of your business,' Mam said. 'He's gone, that's all that matters.'

'I'll tell you where they've sent him,' Bevis yelled vengefully. 'He'll go to the Low Island, to the labour camp. He's a criminal; that's where criminals go. They'll make him work till his back breaks, till his hands bleed. There'll be no food on trays – and –

and—' The list of luxuries was not long. 'And he'll stay there forever, till he dies. No one gets off the island. Next time you hear the Banshee maybe it'll be him and you know what happens then.'

'That's enough.' Mam stood up. 'That's enough, Bevis. We don't talk about it. You,' she looked at Demetria at last, or at least in her direction, 'get upstairs. I'm sick of the sight of you.'

'Aren't you going to thrash her?' Bevis sounded outraged.

'She's got more than a thrashing coming,' Mam said dully. 'She's got to live with this.'

Demetria walked towards the stairs, making a wide circle around Bevis, but he did not touch her again. Instead his voice followed her. 'You've dishonoured this house! You thought you were different, didn't you? You thought you were so special. You thought he liked you, playing games, making kites. *He used you!*'

She lay on the bed, fully dressed, in her coat and shoes, the knitting bag still tied round her waist. She curled up, arms round her head to shut out the hateful words, as she had crouched on the cliff-top, waiting for the soldiers to kill her. But the soldiers had been kind – kind to her. She could not imagine what it had been like when they came to the house and searched every corner. Had they been here, looking in her bed, under it, in the cupboard beside it where she

154

kept her clothes? They must have been through those as well.

But they had not been angry with her. They were sorry for what she had done, for what had been done to her. They had not spoken of dishonour. They had not called her a liar and a toad and – what was the word Mam had used? – a *collaborator*.

They had been angry with Ianto Morgan, angry enough to fire at him. She saw again her last sight of him, staggering, trying to run, the soldier swinging the butt of his weapon.

Had he run for the cliff to leap over it rather than be captured, or to lead them away from her? Or had he forgotten her, left her to her fate while he tried to escape? Why wouldn't he? He hadn't needed her any more, the kite had flown with its coded signal. He had lied to her – the wonderful stories he had told were lies. He did not come from another world, he had not come across the starry sky to help, leaving his children and their mother. He had no children; they were not, as she had imagined, far away on Earth, with its enormous moon that moved the seas, where fish grew leaves and flew through the air. They did not look at the stars at night to find the one where their father had gone, gone forever. That was all lies too.

He had not made the kite for her, he had made it for himself; deceived her into sewing it because his broken thumb could not grip the needle. And the bright tail, red, white and blue, had been a signal. He could not send messages in secret on his blue cards that the censor would see, so he made the code in the kite's tail and took her up to the dangerous cliff-top to fly it, so the enemy would see it.

What enemy?

Who could he have been signalling to? She knelt on the bed and gazed out to the lighthouse, its beam that had come on at sunset, sweeping the strait between the islands. Was that where they had sent him as Bevis had said, for the terrible thing he had done? Ianto Morgan had thought it a terrible punishment to be sent to the High Island; how much worse must the Low Island be?

He deserved it. He had not cared what happened to her. All he had wanted was to fly the kite with its secret message.

And yet –

He hadn't been very secret about it. The cliff-top was in full view of the town. From what she had seen of the lie of the land up there, five minutes more walking would have taken them out of sight.

He hadn't needed her with him. If he'd really only wanted her to sew the fabric he could have told her it was a scarf or a neck cloth. The kite had been for her, surely it had. He had wanted to show her what it meant to fly.

And that hadn't been a lie. He had told her of flight, and shown her what it was, and for those brief moments up there on the cliff in the wind and sunshine, she had believed, as the kite swooped and circled and danced at the end of the line that thrummed in her hands, that a living creature could take to the sky and stay there.

13

Teacher hadn't said she might not talk. She was working on whole stockings now and unless she forgot all she'd painfully learned when she sweated over the heels, there was no reason to work in silence; but no one spoke to her.

She had been afraid of the questions, eager and gloating, about what happened yesterday. No one asked. Stephane would not have gloated but Stephane was not asking either. Demetria, afraid to speak first, waited for Stephane to say something. Stephane knitted silently. She did not strike up a conversation with anyone else to show Demetria that she was being ignored. In fact, no one was speaking much. The sawing and hammering from the next room sounded much louder than usual. Every time she raised her head someone was sure to be looking her way, out of the tail of an eye or from under drooping lids.

They were doing what the adults did, not talking

about it, the way they did not talk about the prison island or the Politicals. It was not simply that they were not talking to her; they would not talk *about* her. The thing that had happened up there on the cliff would never be talked about. And now that Ianto Morgan had gone it was as though he had never been there. He would be forgotten; he was being forgotten now. That was how they did it. By not talking about him they were making him forgotten.

But no one else had known him. They could not really forget him by themselves because they had not known him. She was the only one who had known Ianto Morgan well enough to remember him; to the rest he was just another Political who had stepped out of line. So long as she was not allowed to talk about him, the forgetting would soon be done.

No one else would ever know the things he had told her, the stories – the *lies*. Had she known him after all? Or had she known only the lies he told her? She had not repeated everything to the soldiers; they had not asked. And they had not asked her what she had told him.

At that thought she gave such a jolt that a dozen stitches slipped from her needle and she had to scoop them back before Teacher, pacing, pacing, came to look at her work. Not that she had been able to tell him much, but he had always been asking questions, always disappointed that she knew so little; about the drifts, and the logs – where they came from, where they went. Even so, he'd known more about that than she had. What had he said? *This whole planet was mapped and named before anyone ever set foot on it.* Lies. *There used to be an observatory up here once . . . on the far side of the peak . . . one of the first things to go.* How could he have known about the observatory? Easy. He'd made it up. Another lie, like the fish with leaves. Huge dishes, he had said; metres, tens of metres across. All his lies were huge: the dishes, the moon, sea creatures bigger than boats, high buildings, great bridges and forests –

He had said that he never hit his children. Well, the corporal had told her he had no children.

But he had never hit *her*.

That was only because he had wanted to trick her into helping him.

But he had smiled and called her Dede, the way, perhaps, her father would have done, because he liked the name. He had liked her. She could not believe that he had not liked her.

The sun was bright on the wave crests out beyond the mole, and in the distance the fishing boats were riding home. At the midday break when they were all turned outside, everything seemed to be all right again. The boys were kicking a ball around; a game of hop-toad started up in one free corner. Demetria took her place at the end of the line and no one told her not to. Tall Audrey was in front of her, but in the school yard

Audrey did not have the space to make those unbeatable leaps. She had little advantage over the others. When she came back from the end of her turn, Demetria set off in her wake, bounding from circle to circle until she came to the end of the course, Audrey's last circle. She stopped, calculated, and threw the pebble. It went further than she had meant, but she might just reach it with extra effort. She got ready to spring. Brendan Coveney walked across and casually kicked the pebble out of range. Brodie, who was waiting for it, picked it up and threw it, not violently but contemptuously, over the wall.

Then they went back to their ball game. No one said anything. One of the little girls piped up, 'I've got another one,' threw her pebble and skipped after it. She did not get very far but already the line was re-forming behind her. Demetria stood watching. If she stayed out of the game the Coveney brothers had won, but what would happen if she joined it? What would the other girls do?

They knew what was good for them. As she started for the back of the line she saw Bevis there before her, arms folded, feet apart, not looking at her – not looking at anything; being looked at. He was not there to defend her, he was making sure that he was seen to stop her playing. The girls were silent in the line; no one would look at her.

She wanted to shout at him, *This won't work. You'll make them remember what happened. No one*

161

will forget if you make them remember. But Bevis was beyond working that out for himself. His sister had shamed the family and she was going to pay for it. He was going to make sure that she got more than the thrashing he believed she deserved – as Mam had promised. She thought, in sudden amazement, He's stupid. He's a fool, and she found her fists clenching, jaw tensing. She longed to take a run at him, butt him in the guts, kick him, pummel his smug self-righteous face until he howled, and she was shocked, because girls did not do the hitting. That was what boys did, that was how they arranged things although they were so stupid. She could not recall one interesting, intelligent thing that Bevis had ever said or done, but it was Bevis who would be a man, own the house, keep his wife and children in order with his fists; Bevis and the Coveney brothers and Devlin. Devlin?

She looked to where he was running about with the others. *Defend me, Devlin*. But he had not had a friendly word for her, had not intervened when Brendan Coveney had kicked the pebble away and Brodie had thrown it out of the yard.

Ianto Morgan had intervened when the Coveneys had set on her at the beach. She remembered his angry words: thug, bully, brat. She remembered Brodie's answer: *Don't you know we could have you shot?*

And he had been shot. In spite of the sunshine she went cold all over, trembling, as she had trembled yesterday in the barracks. Why hadn't she asked herself before how it was that the soldiers had reached them so quickly, up on the cliff? They must have been on the way, long before Ianto Morgan got the kite airborne. Someone had told them who those distant figures were; the island girl who looked like every other island girl, and the Political who could have been any Political.

The one o'clock hooter sounded across the strait. The poor devils had finished their slop, he had said, and now, if Bevis were right, he was over there on Low Island with them, one of the poor devils, working till his hands bled and his back broke – there till he died unless in mad despair he tried one night to swim for it, when the Banshee would wail and the lighthouse would go out and he would drown in the darkness if he weren't shot first.

Serve him right. He was an evil man, the sergeant had said. Evil? What was evil? The word had a hateful sound to it.

They filed indoors and Demetria took up her knitting again. The afternoon ground wearily on. No one was talking now, after what had happened in the yard. The carpentry noises in the next room had stopped too. All that could be heard was the Master's voice – he must be giving a map lesson on drifts – and the steady tread as Teacher patrolled the rows. Demetria thought of the story of the mermaid who swam into a fisherman's net. Hadn't she herself swum into a net, and wasn't she now paying for it, she who had thought she was special and had tried to be different?

The house was empty when she came home. Bevis always lingered on the quayside after school. Mam sometimes went to other women's houses when her hair needed doing, and they would wash and plait each other's. Afterwards they would sit knitting together. Demetria often wondered what they talked about, especially Mam. Now they must all be strenuously *not* talking about yesterday, Mam knowing, as Bevis did not, that yesterday must be forgotten, concealed, like a dropped stitch retrieved. Demetria did not think that Mam would be sitting with other women today. Perhaps she was just avoiding Demetria, still sick of the sight of her.

She went out into the garden, down the path, to the shed. The door was ajar. She pushed it open and looked in. It was empty. She had never known what Ianto Morgan had in there except the bed, the table, the chair, the basin and bucket that they had set up before he came. Now even those had gone. The place was as empty as it had been for the few hours between their moving out the gardening tools and the arrival of the furniture, bare and cold. He had never had any heating. The shed had forgotten him already. It smelt of damp stone, not as though someone had lived in it for six weeks.

Then, in the corner, behind the door where no one

would see them, she noticed scratches on the wall; not accidental marks, but deliberately cut on stone with a stone. An eye, like the ones painted on the fishing boats; a face, drawn the way a child would do it – a circle, two dots for eyes, two dots for nostrils, and a smile, a scribble of hair; a fish; a whole stone covered in lines crossing each other like a woven plaid. They were all clumsy, the work of someone with crude materials who could not grip with his broken thumb.

Further along was another fish, a slake by the look of it, with its single tusk. But he'd given it legs, like little twigs, and it seemed to be covered with tongues of hair as if he did not know how to draw scales. No, they were not scales, they were leaves. It had leafy arms too, stretched out on either side. He had drawn what he could not describe: a bird.

Demetria knew what the sergeant would have said: 'It's just part of his lying. He made it up to deceive you.' Badly drawn though it was, it did not look made up. It was too plain. She could see how, with those leafy arms – wings – spread, it might swim in the air as the kite had done.

She did not want to go back to the house to wait for Mam and Bevis, in case Bevis returned first. Mam had said she was not to be thrashed, but Bevis might have other ideas. Those long thin sticks the pulses grew up would suit him nicely – he had used them before. Whatever she did now would be wrong. What she had done would not be forgotten at home. In a way, Ianto Morgan would always be in the shed and her betrayal would not go away. Instead she went out of the gate, down the street, down the path to the beach.

From the water's edge where they had played duxendrakes she could see the peak, brightly sunlit although it was cloudy down there. The waves rolled lazily in, almost as they did in summer. She did not want to go back home, she did not want to go back to school tomorrow, tomorrow and tomorrow, forever, until she was as old as Audrey, old enough to leave, and work alongside Mam until she was ready to be married. She did not want to be married.

She did not want to see her children hit. Oh, to be somewhere else, where no one was ever hit. What was it like up there beyond the cliffs and the sheep fields – beyond the peak? *There used to be an observatory up here once*. Liar. If it had been as huge as he claimed there must be something left. One day she would go and look and find nothing, the proof of his deceit. Why not go now? Why wait and hope?

But if she did not come home, wouldn't she be searched for? Not because anyone was worried about her but because she ought to be in her home and she was not. The cliff might be the first place they would look.

And if she went up there now it would be growing dark before she could come back – even before she reached the top perhaps. Then what would she see? Little more than the grass beneath her feet. What had they seen before? The distant sheep and, far out to sea, a whale, that solitary log on its lone voyage through the strait.

He had always been so interested in the logs – where they came from, where they went. Where was that log now? No one had gone out to get it. If the fishing boats had been in dock someone might have tried, but they had all been out, riding Kepler for burl or sarling. The log would have gone on, into the strait, past the Low Island and then out into the ocean on its mysterious journey. *What goes around comes around*. Would it have returned one day or would it reach another island, like theirs but far away, to be taken captive there, speared and chained and dragged ashore?

Without noticing she had started to walk home again, up the beach, towards the path. She had been stupid even to think of the cliff – there was nowhere to go, ever, except home, back to Mam and Bevis who would not forgive her. And she would have to live, unforgiven, until some man, who was a boy as yet, came to claim her and she unplaited her hair as a bride and walked with it loose over her shoulders, through the streets, for the only time in her life.

Every time Mam washed her hair and twisted it, still wet, into the twenty-seven plaits, she dreamed of that moment of freedom, the first and last, imagining her hair like a cloak, sweeping behind her. But who would want her now?

It was only later, when she was in bed, that her loose confused thoughts began to gather together – thoughts of the logs and the drifts and of what Ianto Morgan had said about swimming: *Anyone can swim. Even I can.* Was that what he had been planning, right from the start? To watch for a log that was travelling too far from shore to be captured, to swim out to it, climb on its back and let Tycho carry him away into the ocean? She had been lying there, watching the lighthouse, wishing that he had never been sent to them, had never told her that there were other ways of living; for even if he had made them up, he had lived them himself, hating the island way. Before he came it had just been how things were and now she could not bear to think that they might be different, but never for her.

And all the time he had been working out a way to escape and leave her behind.

Or would he have taken her with him, come back for her even?

She curled up, knees to chin, and told herself a story in which she was on the beach one day and Ianto Morgan came down and stood beside her and said, 'There's a log out there, if we can swim to it . . .' and she said proudly, 'I've been practising.'

But she could not swim. Of course he had been lying when he told her it was nonsense that women and girls could not swim. He'd said that because he'd wanted her to try, and drown; or had not cared if she did.

But she could not believe that. He had been her friend. As she fell asleep she felt herself slipping easily through the sea towards the log that was coming to fetch her and carry her away, riding Tycho over the ocean.

14

It took her a while to notice something that yesterday she had been too distracted to take in. Yesterday she had been hoping desperately that everything would be all right. Now she knew that it would not; she might not play hop-toad with the other girls, and no one would speak to her, not even Stephane. Bevis and Devlin and the Coveneys would see to that.

At noon she turned her back on the yard and sat on the wall, looking out over the quayside, knitting. It was not schoolwork; she was making herself a new undershirt for next winter, hating it even as she knitted it. It was already stiff and scratchy and repeated washing would not soften it, but it was a simple tube shape and she could look around as she slipped the stitches over her needles. That was when she noticed it.

There were plenty of people about, but where were

the Politicals? Demetria remembered, unwillingly, one of the things she was trying to forget. Coming out of the barracks with the soldier, two days ago, she had seen the silent, waiting islanders on the quayside and somewhere beyond them, movement, soldiers, and a whole group of Politicals being rounded up. It was the first time she had seen so many in one place, since more than two was a conspiracy. She did not even know how many there were in the town altogether, but they had become part of the landscape, walking, sitting in pairs, talking. Now, as she actively looked for them, she finally spotted one, standing alone on the rocks over by the sea grave. She did not know him by sight, she did not know any of them by sight – could not tell one from another. They were all alike. He could have been anyone, he could have been Ianto Morgan, only that was the one person he could not be.

There was another, walking, solitary, along the quayside to watch a boat unloading; another sitting on the mole, staring out to sea. And it did not take her long to work out what had happened; now even two was a conspiracy. If they managed to meet it would have to be in secret. This was all her fault – hers and Ianto Morgan's. Now these lonely men, far from home, would be even lonelier.

The hooter brayed on the Low Island. The sounds of running, jumping feet behind her stopped instantly. She stuffed the knitting into her apron, swung her feet round and dropped into the yard to follow the others indoors.

She was beside Stephane when they hung up their coats. They were the last in; there was no one there to overhear. Demetria said lightly, 'We won't need these much longer.'

When Stephane said nothing she added uncertainly, 'Will we?' That was a question that could be answered if Stephane chose to answer it. She was starting to look round, but then Devlin appeared at the door of the boys' room and he said nothing either. Stephane ducked her head and scuttled to her place. Demetria looked at him imploringly but he was already turning away.

She went to her seat, took up the stocking and began to knit, sure that people were glancing slyly at her, but not daring to look up and find out. She kept her head bent even when Teacher fetched up beside her and held out her hand for the work.

'When you've finished this,' Teacher said, 'you had better start working to increase your speed. You're still very slow. Tomorrow I want a whole stocking done in one day. Hurry up and get this one cast off.'

In one day; well, that was what was expected. In the end it would be a pair in one day, perhaps more. Audrey could already work that fast, although she was on sweaters.

It was a promotion; was it also a punishment? Knitting steadily she could now produce a respectable stocking. If she started making mistakes again, and everyone did when they started speed work, it would be back to peas in her own stockings.

Yesterday she had gone straight home from school. Today she went over the rocks by the mole, directly to the beach. There was a lone Political walking by the water, but when he saw her coming he walked up the sand in a wide detour and went back to the harbour.

'It's not because it's me,' she told herself, knowing that they must all look as alike to the Politicals as the Politicals did to them, bundled shapelessly into their thick coats and heavy shoes, all with their identical blonde plaits hanging behind them. 'Those men must be afraid to talk to *anyone* now.' He did not have to be so obvious about it though.

But she had been right when she said to Stephane that they would not need their coats much longer; or hopefully right. It was not warm but the wind was less piercing even here by the water, and she could feel the sun on her face. When the weather turned hot it would happen fairly quickly, but they were never ready for it. The mothers seemed to agree among themselves about the day when their daughters could shed winter clothes for the thin light shirts and trousers of summer, but it was never soon enough. There were always two or three uncomfortable weeks while they grew daily hotter, stickier, more stifled, under layers of prickly wool, feeling cross and bulky, before the short summer was decreed to have begun. The boys of course decided for themselves.

And in summer the girls got that precious time on the beach after school before the boys turned up and decided that they had had enough freedom. What would happen this year? Would they go away if she tried to join them, spoiling their own fun by trying to spoil hers? Surely they would have forgotten by then, or started to forget, if Bevis and his friends would let them; surely they could all run and jump as before. They could not take off the knitting bags but they tied them under their shirts because there was no one to see, and let the loose clothes make their own breeze as they ran.

Or would they dare to do even that now? She paused, halfway along the beach. It must have been just about here, last year, while they were taking turns to skip over a length of rope Tycho had left for them, that Audrey's friend Josephine had slipped on a slick of seaweed. As she had gone down backwards in a long skid her shirt had whipped up over her head and she had lain flat on the sand like a big stranded fish. They had stood around her, gaping, appalled by the sight of so much bare skin, and then rushed off to the water's edge so that when Josephine disentangled herself and sat up she would not know that they had been looking. But every time Demetria saw a catch of sarling unloaded on the quay, with their smooth white bellies uppermost, she thought of Josephine's long pale body, which became longer, whiter, smoother, more fish-like, the less she remembered what she had actually seen. Then she could not help sneaking a glance at Josephine who, naturally, had no idea what she was thinking. It was Demetria who blushed deeply, knowing what she had in mind.

One day, playing the looking-glass game with Stephane, she said, 'If I showed you . . . would you tell me what I look like . . . somewhere else?'

'Somewhere else?' Stephane said, sitting on the school wall. 'What's wrong with here?'

'No.' Demetria hesitated, ran her hands down her front. 'I mean, underneath. If *you* showed me I'd tell you.'

Stephane's face told her all she needed by way of an answer. If only she dared to look for herself.

Tycho had brought nothing much today, mostly debris, although there was a length of rope as thick as her plait at the top end, and heavy. She could not imagine what she might do with it, but the habit of collecting was too strong for her to leave it. She looped it over her arm and walked on towards the Point. No one else was coming that way. Had the others seen her there and decided to leave her on her own?

She almost wished they would *do* something, so that she could resist. Years ago, she remembered, when she was first at school learning baby things like reading, there had been a big girl, as big as Audrey – although everyone had seemed enormous then. This girl had upset someone, somehow – Demetria had never known the facts – and for weeks had been tormented with pinches and shoves and whispers. The whispers had been the worst of all, she thought, looking back. In the end the girl had cracked and launched herself at the others in the yard, screaming and kicking, until her brother had hauled her off and slapped her until she had calmed down. But if anyone was whispering about Demetria they took care that she did not know it. What she had done called for more than whispers; after Brodie Coveney had thrown the pebble away yesterday, without looking at her, everyone had known what to do. They behaved as though she were not there at all.

Was there time now to get up on to the cliff-top? If she went home it would be to more silence, and the silence of Mam and Bevis in the small cottage was worse than the silence of ninety in the school yard. No one had said anything when she had come in yesterday, late. Bevis hadn't even bothered to clout her. The food had been cold, but it was no worse cold than warm. She left the water's edge, walked up the beach and began to climb.

This was not the way they had come with the kite, but if she went on and up she would soon join their path. That had been steep but firm underfoot. Now she was treading on loose rocks among the grass.

Brittle spikes of last year's dead plants stood above the new spring leaves. The long pliable branches of thorn and scrub had little green and red buds along them.

When she looked round she saw that she was already out of sight of the beach. No one ever came up here, there was no reason to, but she began to wonder what it would be like in summer with the leaves out, the grass green and thick, with flowers in it. Nearby she could hear the bubbling trickle of running water, and then she saw it. Over and around the stones, in the grass, a little stream was running, fresh out of the hillside like a miniature version of the Blackwater that cut down through the town.

She began to follow it, not noticing that instead of going up she was moving downhill. The streamlet had cut a bed for itself. She was in a narrow gully and the rocky sides rose higher until they were level with her chest and so close together that she had to sidle. The downward slope was becoming steeper.

About to turn back, she saw where the stream was going. Ahead was the sea. There was no room to lean down and look along the gully, which was now almost a tunnel, but she could see that in less than two metres it would widen again. She forced herself between the overhangs, becoming wedged more than once by the bulk of her coat, and then she was through. The effort had been worth it.

She was only just the other side of the Point at the

end of the beach but the stream had carved out a little cove that was quite cut off. At her feet was a rocky basin with sides that went straight down into the water except for one place where it sloped to a shelf, level with the surface. Shallow waves slopped gently at the rim. The stones beneath her feet were small and loose, and she lost her balance, skied down the last few metres, grabbing at the rocks and, painfully, a thorn bush, coming to a halt on the shelf.

When her heart stopped thumping she crouched and looked round. The place was completely hidden; no one could see into it from anywhere above, and only someone scaling the rocks from the beach would discover it. Perhaps no one ever had. She had never heard it spoken of, even as a place to stay away from; it was hers, her own private world, Planet Demetria.

The sun was on the sea, she could see right to the bottom, green weedy rocks and clear green water. Slender shapes darted among the weeds, probably slake. She dipped her hand in and two or three of them swam up to investigate. She felt their tusks, an inquisitive tickling against her fingers, then they dived and went peacefully about their business.

She watched them flicker and swoop in the green depths. How easily they moved, like the kite. Was this how birds moved in the air? And if the slake could skim around so easily, why couldn't she?

Because she couldn't. *Why* not? Why couldn't girls swim? Because the men and the boys and the mothers and the teachers said so, so no one ever tried, because it was well known that there was something wrong with women, something inside them that made them sink. That was why they were never allowed out in the boats. It was not true, he had said. If she were ever to find out, this would be the perfect place to put it to the test, where nobody could see.

The cove did not seem to be very deep. She picked up a pebble and let it fall, watching it slip through the water and glide to a rest at the bottom, attracting half a dozen slake. Deeper than it looked, then, but the water was sheltered and very calm. If she lowered herself in, keeping a hold of the edge of the shelf, she would soon find out if she could even float. If the warnings were true and she started to sink, she could easily get out again.

Or could she? She had overheard enough talk of undertows to know that calm water could be treacherous, and she thought of the pale bloated corpses cast up on the beach among the seaweed, but if she had some kind of lifeline, fixed to something stable, she would be safe. The coil of rope was still over her arm. It looked immensely strong but it was too thick to knot. If she were to venture into those green depths she would need something that she could attach to land at one end and herself at the other.

There was the gnarled thorn bush growing out of the rocks just above her that had taken her weight

179

when she had clutched it on the way down. She reached up and pulled at it. It stayed firmly rooted. She tugged, then swung from the trunk. That would do for an anchor, the other end of the line could go under her arms. The rope would not do, but it could not be long before Tycho sent her something more suitable. She coiled it up in her knitting bag in case she should find a use for it later.

She would have to take her coat off, and her shoes. If she went in fully dressed she would certainly sink and going home soaked would make even Mam say something, so she would have to remove her frock and sweater . . . and her trousers? Right down to her undershirt and drawers – oh, no, that was unthinkable.

Her hand trailed in the water again. It wasn't so very cold, she told herself, and in a few weeks' time it would be almost warm, and soon after that she would have her thin summer clothes.

If it turned out that girls could swim, why, there was no limit to how far she could go.

15

The weather did grow warmer but only gradually, one fine day being followed by a week of cold winds, blustering showers and a sun that showed only rarely between clouds.

Now that Demetria had found her cove she could not wait for the moment when she could put her daring plan into action, although if it turned out that Ianto Morgan was right, that girls could float and swim, there was no one she could tell.

She wondered if she could have told Stephane once. Stephane was no more than a silent presence beside her in school now. But didn't she owe it to Ianto Morgan to prove, even if he never knew it, that he was right? No – if he was right he would know that anyway; she would be proving that she believed him. After all, he had been telling the truth about the kite. She thought of him every time she heard the bell and the hooter, which was all the time.

Was he over there on the Low Island, as Bevis had claimed?

At night she lay hoping that the Banshee would remain silent.

While she waited for the warm weather she haunted the beach on sore feet – the speed knitting was going as badly as she had feared. Tycho was taking its time about bringing her a lifeline. There was more of the thick rope and a great tangle of net that lay on the beach like a heap of weed. She picked over the net, wondering if she could unravel it, but it had already been badly damaged. The fibres could not be relied upon to hold.

One day brought a small log fall. She took a sack and went down for bark. The Coveneys were everywhere, ignoring her as usual, but it seemed that whenever she had her eye on a particularly big piece a Coveney would suddenly be there before her, shoving her aside, not deliberately but as if they had not seen her because she was not there. Bevis and Devlin collared a dolphin. Devlin had been kind to her once. Now he looked straight through her.

There was something in the shallows. At first she thought it was a sea creature, bright orange, slithering in the surf, and approached it with caution. Then she saw that it was some kind of twine, a generous length of it. She dared not pick it up in case someone else decided that they had seen it first. Instead she made herself carry the sack of bark home and did not go back until she was sure that everyone else would have gone. The orange rope was still there and she gathered it in. She had never seen anything quite like it before, slightly hairy, thin and very strong. It was difficult to tell what it was made of but it did not stretch and the strands did not part. Tycho had brought her what she needed.

It was four weeks since she had found the cove and it had taken all her willpower not to return there, for she was always afraid that someone might follow her. It was so close to the beach, just a climb over those rocks at the Point, and no one must know what she was planning to do. But four was a special number of weeks. Ianto Morgan had had a word for it – a month. It was a month since she had found the cove and lost her friend. It was time to do something; Tycho approved.

She stuffed the twine into her apron and went home. Tomorrow was Senday, market day, she might just take her prize down to the cove and hide it there while no one was about. It was too much to hope that tomorrow would be the day when they were allowed into their summer clothes. However hot and uncomfortable they were in school, itching and stuffy, she had to admit that the wind was still very cool, and the boys who rushed around the yard in their shirtsleeves were probably wishing they'd waited.

*

But the next day was cloudless and the wind had dropped.

'Get the pulses sown this morning,' Mam said to Bevis before she went down to market. 'And you –' she had not spoken Demetria's name since *that* day – 'hoe the root garden, *after* you've finished in the house. And don't forget to darn your stockings. You've gone through the heels again.'

At that rate it might be midday before she got away, a time when people began to leave the market and walk on the beach. She did not want anyone about when she visited her cove.

The soil around the growing root crops was dry and hard, the weeds cemented in. The hoe handle gave her blisters and the sun sent sweat meandering down her back. She did not have to wear her coat in the garden, but the winter clothes felt heavy and dirty, the frock rasping at her neck and pulling under the arms, her trousers tight round her waist, stockings nipping her legs above the knee where the drawstrings were gathered to hold them up. Her feet were swollen inside her shoes, which were filling with gritty dust, and the apron, loaded with the orange twine and the rope as well as her knitting, was always in the way, banging against her knees. Once Mam would have noticed the extra contents and demanded to know what she had in there. Now she did not even look.

Bevis had put in the pulses and set up the pyramids of canes long before she had finished hoeing, but he

184

hung around in the kitchen – probably, she thought, to make sure that she did finish. The gardening tools were back in the shed now. When she looked through the louvres while putting the hoe away, she saw him prowling up and down the rows, hoping to find a weed still standing, so he could order her out again. She wished he would go away as he usually did, down to his friends in the town. She did not want to leave the house first in case he followed her. Even if he didn't he might see which way she went and go exploring later, for himself. The cove would be ruined if Bevis found it. He would never be able to squeeze between those overhangs but he might work out that there was another way round, over the Point.

The least he could do was make sure that she was never allowed there again. 'It's too dangerous,' she could imagine him saying, loudly. 'She could be drowned. I have to protect my sister.'

As she stood in the shed she traced the crude drawing of the slake with legs – the bird that Ianto Morgan had scratched on the stone. If it turned out that she could swim, perhaps she could fly too.

Bevis went away at last. Demetria stood at the garden gate and watched until he was past the second bend and definitely heading into town. Then she went indoors to fetch her coat, which she did not want but dared not leave off in case Mam came home and saw it. You wore your coat until you were told you need not wear your coat, it was that simple.

And again she thought, as she thought so often these days, about so many things: *Why?*

The beach was still deserted when she came down the path. She skirted the sand, struck out uphill again until she found the stream, then followed it. This time she took off her coat before she reached the overhangs and slid through easily, and there below her was the cove, as she had last seen it and had been picturing it ever since; the cool stones, the green water. The thorn bush was in bloom now. Little flowers starred the grass. Spring had come earlier to this sheltered place in the sun, out of the wind. There were even some hop-toads on the ledge, but they sprang into the water and dived when they felt her footfalls.

She laid the coat on a rock and the knitting bag on top of it. Then, feeling reckless, she unbuckled her shoes, drew off her stockings and sat for happy minutes feeling the smooth stone of the shelf under her hot sore feet. There was dust between her toes and the sweat was turning it to mud, she noticed with disgust. Almost without meaning to she slid her feet towards the edge of the shelf and rinsed them in the clear sea-water. It was cooler than she had expected, but coolness was what she wanted, craved.

Why wait for high summer? She was alone, it was a beautiful day and she had the lifeline. She pulled it out of the apron and measured it by eye; five metres, maybe six. The thorn bush offered its sturdy elbow: *Trust me*. She tied one end of the line round it. Girls were not taught rope work but it was impossible not to pick up one or two basics, and she used a knot which she knew would not slip open. She swung on it to make sure and the thorn bush creaked in a resilient way. Neither it nor the line would break.

She sat down again to undress. No one could see her but she did not want to see herself. She hugged her knees and looked at the clothes lying in a dark dusty heap, like something that had washed up on the beach and dried out; sweater, frock, trousers – how much more dare she take off? The air was soft against her skin. She slid out of her drawers and then, last of all, shuddering at the sudden chill and her own daring, the knitted undershirt. She could not bear the thought of it wet, heavy and clinging; it was uncomfortable enough dry.

Her plait lay cold against her spine. She took the loose end of the line and began to fasten it under her armpits, but it did not make her feel secure. If anything went wrong, if it caught on something underwater, the knot would be out of reach between her shoulderblades. She untied it and passed it round her middle instead, tying the double loop knot that was easy to release if you pulled the right end.

And now the water was waiting. She still sat with her knees drawn up under her chin, overcome by the thought of the awful thing that she was going to do; not just thinking the unthinkable but making it happen. Girls could not swim. She would sink. No one went naked, anywhere, not even in private, much less in the open. She even undressed for bed under the tent of her nightshirt, but having got this far she could not give up, knowing that she had defeated herself. The wavelets nibbled coaxingly at her toes. She lay back on the sloping shelf and began to shuffle herself into the water.

It was unbelieveably cold, slipping over her ankles, calves, thighs, like icy stockings, but she kept going, slowly, teeth clenched, trying to ignore the knot where it dug into her back. Then she was too far over the lip of the ledge to stop. A freezing wave slapped her across the belly, she gave a whoop of shock, flung up her arms and went down like a stone.

The line pulled her up short with a brutal jolt under the ribs, punching air out of her lungs in a gush of bubbles. For a second she hung, horizontal, then her head dipped and her legs went up; something was wrong. She pushed against the water with her palms, but she could not bring her feet down. Instead her head and arms swung lower, legs kicking uselessly. The loop of the rope had slipped from her waist to her hips – she had tied it too low, too loose; she was jack-knifed over it. Her fingertips swept the weedy stones as she bucked and swung, bashing against rocks, writhing over and round but always head down in the noose that should have been her lifeline and was now drowning her in a blizzard of bubbles and churning weed.

If she had stopped kicking she might have slipped free. If she had known what she was seeing she would have recognized her own flailing arms and thrashing legs, but she was beyond knowing anything. Demetria Joyce no longer existed, there was nothing human – only a creature, a thing, a sac of bursting skin that struggled in mindless terror on the end of a line like a hooked fish.

Then her clawing fingers engaged with the taut line. She gripped it instinctively, came right-side up and shot to the surface.

At first she could do nothing but cling to the rope, retching and gasping, while draughts of burning air roared down her throat. Her nose was bleeding. She did not notice the cold, all she knew was that she was alive. At last she gripped the shelf and heaved herself on to it. The effort made her vomit up water through nose and mouth and for a long while she lay there, face down, legs still trailing in the water, too weak to move, too shaken.

Slowly she began to think again. The sun was off the cove now, the wind cold on her skin, but she did not want to stir. Only the fear that someone might come over the rocks finally got her moving and she dragged herself to her knees. Every bone of her was bruised – spine, shoulders, elbows, knees – and from the waist down she felt as if she had been sawn into

189

strips. The lifeline, which had done most of the damage, had tightened into a hard knot. Too sore to wriggle out of it she crawled to her apron for the scissors and even with those it was almost impossible to cut.

Refusing to cry but unable to keep herself from whimpering, she pulled on her clothes, starting from habit with her stockings, tying the strings with trembling fingers; ending, also from habit, with her apron. She remembered not to put on her coat until she was through the overhangs, but she was too exhausted to untie the line from the thorn bush. It hung there, vibrantly orange, and mocked her stupidity. She had been told a lie, and had believed it.

Somehow she staggered home, wringing out her dripping plait on the way and hearing once again the hooter from the Low Island as she climbed the path. It was barely two hours since she had set out and in that time she had looked death in the face. She had lived to look away again, but she did not think of that. She felt as if she had been beaten; the sea had beaten her. She was not perfect, not different. She was the same as any other girl or woman.

Mam was at home when she crept into the kitchen. Demetria waited for the sharp eyes to take in the wet hair and other telltale signs. She had no idea how she looked but something must show after all that. If it did, Mam did not notice. She scarcely looked up from her knitting.

'You missed your supper.'

'I went to the beach.' The plait dripped on to the floor. 'I fell in the water.' Her voice was all sighing air. The climb from the cove had finished her off; she could not stay upright a moment longer.

'Can I go to bed? I don't want any dinner.'

'You won't get any. Did all that hoeing wear you out? Not too tired to go playing around, I notice.'

'I feel sick.'

'You've been stuffing yourself, I suppose.'

Stuffing herself with what, seaweed? She had been in such a hurry to get down to the cove she had forgotten about dinner. Still, Mam had not said that she mustn't go to bed, so she hung up her coat and made the final climb to her room.

Undressing again was agony; the clammy clothes were stuck to her, but it was not until she was lying in bed, with the blanket over her head, that she realized just how bad she felt. Her nose and mouth and throat were scoured with sea-water and every breath hurt down to the bottom of her lungs. She could still taste that water, it would be in her nose and on her tongue forever. Every bruise and graze glowed and throbbed and she had not dared to look at the rope burns. She curled on her side, then rolled wincing on to her stomach, the skin over her hip bones scraped raw. When she turned on her back she discovered the fiery weals that would make the hours of sitting in school a misery for days to come. Over she went again.

The plait, hard and cold, still wet, dug into her cheek. She pulled it out straight and laid it across the pillow so that it hung over the low bed head and as she did so she saw, as though it were all happening again, where she had gone wrong.

After all, she had not drowned, she had risen to the surface under her own power. It was the misplaced rope that had kept her down.

But if she threaded it through her plait it could only hold her up; after all, that was why the men on the boats wore their little pigtails so that their mates could grab them if they went overboard. She saw herself lying in the cove, lying *on* the water, with the plait stretched out behind her as she floated.

The pain did not get any less, but as her eyes closed, the bitterness of defeat began to ease.

Perhaps, perhaps, this was another of his stories that would turn out to be true.

16

Two weeks later she trudged home from school in blistering sunshine, and when she went up to her slice of a room she found that Mam had been there before her and gone through the clothes cupboard.

The mothers had decided: summer had begun, or would begin tomorrow. Across the bed lay her two pairs of cotton trousers and two shirts. This meant that she might put them on in the morning and leave out the smothering winter woollens to be washed, patched, darned, put away or even, with luck, replaced.

But none of her summer clothes had been replaced. Her joy at seeing them was dampened by the sight of the same ones from last year, and they had not been new then. Did Mam not think she would have outgrown them, or didn't she care how Demetria looked or how she felt? After the chafing suffocation of the last few weeks she had been dreaming of freedom.

Because she could not tell of her injuries without confessing how she had come by them, the grazes and burns and welts had not been dressed and were healing slowly under the scratchy wool. She had not even had the heart to try anything on before she went to bed, as she usually did.

In the morning she had no choice. She had not grown that much since last year; nothing was exactly tight, not tight enough to split, but there was none of that delightful longed-for looseness, with the shirt swishing airily round her knees. It barely touched them and the sleeves were halfway up to her elbows. The trousers did not cover her ankles as they were supposed to and when she fastened the drawstrings they did not quite reach her waist. That was actually a relief – she was still wearing a belt of bruises.

Surely Mam would say something when she came down to breakfast, but as she went into the kitchen Mam had her back turned, standing at the stove. It was Bevis who looked at her and said, 'No, I told you. She doesn't need anything new.'

He had been wearing his summer clothes for weeks and they were all new. Was the rest of her life at home going to be ordered by Bevis? Was it already? Did he decide what she ate as well as what she wore? Did Mam agree to that or had she stopped caring? Would Bevis decide when she was to be punished, and for what?

She ate her porridge – *that* never changed, summer

194

or winter – tied on her knitting bag and set off down the hill. The sun was already hot; at last she could enjoy it. From the second corner she could see down into the streets below, other girls in their new shirts, brightly white or sometimes striped. Her own was striped but the colours were faded.

In the classroom everything seemed brighter because their clothes were, and their plaits, which had looked so white against their dark winter sweaters, were now only pale yellow, various shades of straw, although by the end of summer they would be bleached to match the shirts. And they were all so slim!

Looking at the sleek, shining heads around her, Demetria ran a hand over her own. The twenty-seven little twists of torment were surprisingly loose and she could feel stray tendrils. When she hiked the plait over her shoulder to inspect it she saw how frayed it had become and it struck her that it was well over a month since it had last been washed and rebraided. In fact, Mam had done it the week before she had gone up to the cliff with Ianto Morgan to fly the kite and that was seven weeks ago.

Much as she hated the hairwashing and the spiteful tweaking of the plaits, she felt her eyes sting. Was Mam never going to do it again? Was she going to be left like this, growing more bristly and unkempt, unless she could manage to do it herself? How could she? No one took care of their own hair. Grown women went to a friend or a relative. She did not even know how long it was when it was loose, she had never seen it. Everything went on behind her and, literally, over her head.

If she untied the plait herself and made a fearful mess of winding it up again Mam would have to do something about it . . . wouldn't she? Demetria heard Bevis's toneless voice laying down the law: *No, leave it. Let her wear it like that.*

What were the other girls thinking? No wonder they kept giving her those swift glances. Once she could have asked Stephane, 'Tell me how I look.' Then she thought, Perhaps I still can. It's worth a try.

She did not attempt to join in the hop-toad game at dinner break but leaned against the wall, knitting and gazing out over the harbour. She was still trying to avoid sitting more than she had to, but if anyone had noticed they had not mentioned it – or not to her.

At the end of the afternoon when the rest of the girls went scrambling across the rocks to the beach, she followed. They fanned out over the sand, leaping and twirling, arms spread, plaits swinging. After Josephine's mishap last summer no one had said anything to anyone, but word must have got around, for two days later they had been all back in their winter clothes again although there still had been two or three weeks of hot weather to run. Nobody was going to make *that* mistake this year, especially not on the first day. They kept their knitting bags tied firmly over their shirts and Josephine's was pulled tighter than anyone's, almost cutting her in two. Demetria's shirt was too skimpy to fly up, but she did not want to look different, especially now. She swivelled her bag round to the back like the others and ran to the middle of the group.

They were already starting their favourite beach game of trawling. The first person to be caught joined hands with the catcher and they both went after the next girl, adding a new link to the trawl-line until there was only one person left free. This was a game where they could not ignore her. If they chose not to catch her she could still run and dodge and enjoy the fun – but she would be the last one left, they would have to let her win, and that would spoil it for them as much as for her.

For a while she could not tell if it were her own turn of speed that kept her off the line, or whether they were taking care to avoid her, but just as she was feeling sure that this was what was happening, her plait was seized and when she looked round there was Stephane, holding out her hand to draw her on to the line, and she was happy again, running with the others, all forgiven, forgotten, her hand in Stephane's, like the old days.

There was only leggy Audrey left now. As they thundered down the beach to encircle her, Audrey, the winner, decided to give them a run for their money, skipped sideways into the shallows and raced away again, towards the town. The whole chain wheeled and changed direction, shrieking with laughter.

But they had gone only a few steps when the trawl-line began to falter, slow down and break up. Ahead of them Audrey had slithered to a stop at the sight of the boys, coming over the rocks to the beach. They were not quite marching in step but they moved purposefully, all together. Demetria felt Stephane's warm hand unclasp, the girl on the other side let go a moment later, and before she fully understood what was happening they were all running again, away from her, before the brothers arrived and saw that they were disobeying the order that no one had spoken aloud.

Demetria stood alone by the edge of the sea, watching the fleeing girls, the advancing boys. She did not know what they would do. Ignore her? Chase her away? Attack her? There were so many of them. She turned and, feeling herself starting to shake, walked up the sand and away from the sea, towards the path home. They did not come after her but she could sense them standing there in a silent group at the foot of the path, leaving her to work out what might happen if she played with their sisters again, spreading her dishonour through respectable families.

Why did they *care* so much? It was the Politicals who were suffering, not the islanders. They had all gone back to being locked in at night, released in the morning, checked on at noon. And there were more soldiers from the mainland now to do the locking up and checking. They even had a patrol boat. They were a constant reminder of what had happened and why. No one would ever forget.

Did the Politicals hate her too? They had understood how things were. They had not needed many guards because the island itself was their gaol, the islanders their gaolers. And then Ianto Morgan had come along and wrecked everything, with her help. He had made himself her friend because he was unhappy and lonely and missing his children. He had never told her that, but she had known what it was to miss someone who went away and never came back. Anjelica. And she knew even better now.

The following morning, sitting next to Stephane in class, she said as casually as she could, 'That was fun on the beach yesterday, wasn't it?'

Stephane said nothing.

'Shall we go again after school?'

Stephane bit her lip. Demetria pressed on.

'Shall we play hop-toad at dinner break?'

Stephane began counting her stitches.

'On Senday, after market, shall we walk on the mole?'

Stephane raised her hand to call the teacher. Everyone looked. Usually you waited for Teacher to come to you.

There was still that thing that Demetria had thought was worth trying. It was not worth it, but anyway she shoved her face between Stephane and her knitting. 'Tell me how I look.'

'What is the matter?' Teacher said.

'Demetria's annoying me,' Stephane said. There was a collective gasp. No one ever complained to Teacher about another girl. Stephane's face turned a dull red.

Teacher sighed and looked out of the window, not at either of them. 'Go and stand at the front, Demetria.'

She gathered up her knitting and limped to the table where Teacher sat, facing the class. It was supposed to be a terrible shame to be sent to stand there where everybody could see you, but Demetria was happy to stand. She let her eyes go out of focus until all she could see was a pale blur of heads and knitted faster and faster, without once looking down at her work, never dropping a stitch. Now she really knew how things were.

When school ended she was out of the yard before the others had left the building, over the rocks and on to the sand, running as if pursued. When she reached the far end by the Point they were not even in sight yet. Perhaps they were all going to exile themselves from the beach, leaving her in possession. Let them – silly fools, cowards. She would not be there either. In a moment she was up among the scrub, hidden, following her stream, slipping easily between the overhangs, down to the cove.

The orange twine still hung from the thorn bush where she had left it as she had crawled away from the scene of her defeat. The cut end was lying across the shelf, waiting.

She kicked off her shoes and pulled off her clothes in seconds, this time standing upright, uncaring. She twitched the plait forwards and threaded the twine through it from the end, up to her head and back again. The brilliant strand looked so pretty, woven among the pale coils. What a shame they could not all decorate their hair like that, it would be so easy. *Why* couldn't they? In case it made them happy?

When she tested the water with her foot she was pleasantly surprised to find that it was much warmer than she had expected. This time she went in backwards, keeping a firm grasp with her elbows on the shelf, and then pushed herself out into the water until her arms were at full stretch. She did not sink. Her face was underwater and her open eyes saw the green depths as clear as glass, right down to the little slake nosing among the weeds and the hop-toads skittering on the sand. Her plait hung down straight with the orange line glowing in it. She closed her eyes, let go of the shelf and turned over, spreading her arms.

She was floating.

For a little while she lay there, lay *on* the water, with the sun warming her front and something else warming her from inside; the truth. He had not lied. Everyone else had lied but not Ianto Morgan, her friend. Women did not sink when they went into the sea. They were not made wrong. She was drifting, as light as a leaf on the surface, drifting –

She was drifting out of the cove, but before panic could capsize her the orange twine tugged gently at the plait. From starting, dangerously, to sit up, she simply turned over again, knowing that she was safely moored, and began to make those slow scything strokes and deliberate kicks that she had seen men do when they dived from the mole, and the rocks of the cove came closer again. She was not floating any more, she was swimming.

Within minutes she was sorry that the line was so short, that she could go such a little distance without it pulling her back, but she was grateful to it. However still and calm the sea looked, Tycho had tried invisibly to drag her away from the shore. If not for the orange twine she would have been lost, borne away on the drift, perhaps sucked under and swallowed. She did not know how hungry Tycho could be.

From beyond the Point she heard voices; the brothers had come on to the beach, but they could not be getting any fun from it because the sisters were not there to be driven away. Unhurriedly she climbed out and sat on the shelf, letting the sun dry her while she unthreaded the twine, listening to the low surly muttering on the other side of the rocks: Brodie Coveney, Brendan, Bevis and Devlin, Audrey's brother, Josephine's three brothers; bullies, thugs, brats.

She could hear that they were throwing stones into the water, arguing about whose went furthest, grunting with effort, but they didn't know about duxendrakes. They did not make their pebbles spin sweetly, kiss the water and leap again. Whatever they threw went down and stayed down.

When the voices died away she put on her clothes and went home. If Tycho wanted her then she wanted something in exchange – a longer lifeline so that she could swim out of the cove, test herself in open water, dive to the bottom and join the slake in their explorations. She might never fly in the air, like Ianto Morgan's birds, but she could fly in the sea.

17

Tycho sent her a knot of fishing line which she patiently untangled. Using her fingers she crocheted it up into a thick cord and used it to extend the orange twine. Now she had thirty metres of freedom, to float and swim, to tread water and dive down to the floor of the cove among the waving weeds. She could hold her breath and sit on a rock while the slake played among her fingers, the hop-toads skipped over her toes, and she looked up at the place where she had almost died, just two metres below the surface.

She might have made the sea her friend but she knew she could never trust it. It was a long while before she began to swim out of the cove, testing herself against the pull of the drift and at last, when she was sure that the beach was deserted, venturing beyond the end of the Point into open water, before the tug on her plait reminded her: *That's far enough for now.*

When she saw the boys diving from the mole after school, splashing and floundering in the murky soup of the harbour, she knew that she could outswim any of them.

She found things on the bed of the cove: a knife, coins, an oilskin pouch of the kind that seamen kept their valuables in. This made her wonder if perhaps other people had once known about the place and come down there, like her, to be alone. They might come again. She stowed everything in the knitting bag and kept the lifeline in there too, in case anyone should see it tied round the thorn bush and take it away or, worse, start to wonder who had left it there. She kept back part of her dinner each day and put it in the oilskin pouch to keep fresh so that there was always something to eat when she came out of the sea and sat on the ledge to dry in the sun.

But she did not need the cove to be alone in. She was alone at school and alone at home. Using her plait as a mooring rope had turned it into a scrubby, unravelling skein of threads, dirty and matted, and it was always damp, but Mam never said anything. No one would tell her what her head looked like, but she could feel the twenty-seven braids loose with four or five centimetres of growth. Her scalp itched and scratching loosened more tendrils and she could *see* them. They curled, like the ones on the pulse plants, into little coils and springs, and she realized why her hair had to be plaited so tightly. Curls went where they liked. That could not be allowed. In the end she could stand it no longer.

'Mam, will you wash my hair?'

Mam was cutting out cloth, a garment for Bevis, no doubt. He had gone out, but Mam looked round nervously before saying, without meeting her eyes, 'It doesn't need doing yet.'

Mam was afraid of Bevis. It was Bevis who ordered that his sister should have no new clothes, that she should be friendless at school. Now he ordained that her hair, the one thing that no one could fail to notice, should be left unwashed and ungroomed.

'Please, Mam, it does. It feels terrible. It's been months—'

'Months? What do you mean, months?'

'Weeks,' Demetria said quickly. 'Weeks and weeks.'

Mam laid down the shears. 'Where's your brother?'

'He's out. *Mam*—'

Mam pulled up a stool to the sink, pushed Demetria down on to it and wrapped a towel round her. Demetria forgot how she hated the trapped feeling and leaned her head back, the rim of the sink cool against her neck, but as Mam went to the stove for hot water the garden gate banged open, there were footsteps on the path and Bevis stood in the doorway.

'What are you doing?'

Mam put the kettle down.

'I told you to leave her alone.' Bevis strode across

206

the kitchen. 'She's a dirty, lying collaborator. Let her be dirty.'

Mam was still at the stove. She said meekly, 'Do you want your supper, Bevis?'

'Keep it. There's logs coming in, a great load. We'll be at it till dark.' He went over to Mam and wagged his finger under her nose. 'Remember what I said. Let her alone.'

'But, Bevis . . . what's to become of her?'

As though she would never have her hair washed again, never have new clothes, never be spoken to, not even fed, until she withered away and stopped troubling them. Demetria, still sitting on the stool, wound in the towel, stared from one to the other. She felt like a package left on the quay by the mail-boat, that no one would claim, no one wanted.

Bevis had no answer. He barely looked at Demetria as he turned and went out. How tall he was now, how big his boots were, how hard and red his fists. When he had gone she tottered off the stool.

'Mam, get me out of this then.'

Mam was looking out of the window, the one that faced the strait, where Demetria had looked out that long-ago night and seen their guest, 37250 Ianto Morgan, walking in the street while the Banshee wailed.

'*Mam* – the towel.'

Mam did not look round. Between them, on the table, lay the sewing shears, the half-cut cloth.

Demetria worked her elbows in furious silence until she loosened the towel and shrugged it off, leaving it in a heap on the floor. With one hand she seized the plait and raised it above her head. With the other she picked up the shears and brought the blades together.

She had thought that one swift slash would do it but the hair was so thick that it took three, four, five chops to get it off. By the time Mam realized what the sound was, and looked round, it was all over. Demetria stood for a moment, holding the shears in her right hand, and eleven years, eight months of hair in the left. Then she put them down quite gently on the table and went out by the street door, closing it quietly behind her. She was too shocked to make a scene. She had reached the first bend in the road before she started running.

She headed for the cove. Where else was there to go?

People were already gathering on the beach and she saw that some of the men had dinghies. That meant that the fishing boats were out; no one would be able to pursue an errant log very far. And then she saw what was coming, a huge flotilla, a perfect summer log fall, every one a whale, enough to keep the town busy as Bevis had said, from now until it grew dark.

She went down the path a little way, then turned and struck out through the fields until she came to the rough hilly land at the foot of the cliff. She could not hear the consoling murmur of her stream above the racket from the beach, shouting, cheering, splashing, but she found it soon enough and followed it down to the cove.

When she came to the overhangs she paused and climbed up for another look just as the logs were drawing level, close-packed as if Tycho itself were herding them, and there, a little way behind, was a single rogue whale, steering itself, aloof from the herd that was heading for captivity, out into the strait; the one that would get away.

She dropped back to the bed of the stream and went on down to the cove. How long could she stay here? How long before she had to take her shorn head back to Mam and Bevis and the scandalized eyes of the town? It felt so strange and light, the loose ends flicking around her face, nothing behind her dragging her head back.

Now she had nothing to fasten her lifeline to, but it would be madness anyway to swim with half the neighbourhood swarming along the shoreline on the other side of the Point. Perhaps she could just slip into the water and lie there, dive down and sit on her rock among the weeds away from the noise – safe at least until she had to go home. It would be so peaceful, drifting down there . . .

She had bent to take off her shoes and as she straightened up she heard a shout from above and another from behind. Staring down at her was Brodie Coveney, standing where she had stood just now to look at the logs. She must have been seen during that short time she had been visible from the beach. And on the rocks, that she had hoped no one would ever climb, was Bevis.

There was no time even to think. She stepped into the water.

She had not meant them to believe that she was drowning, but as the sea closed over her head she realized that if she swam underwater for a little way they would be looking in the wrong place when she did break the surface. Would they dive in and try to save her – surely even Bevis didn't want her dead, she was more fun alive and miserable like the Politicals – or swim after her with powerful male strokes? What if they did? She could outswim anyone.

She had never meant to swim in her clothes but she found that there was so little slack in the outgrown garments that she hardly noticed she was wearing them. The apron was a nuisance but she could deal with that in a moment.

When she had to come up for air she paused, treading water, and saw that she had done the right thing. People were streaming away from the beach and the logs, up on to the rocks where two or three boys, Bevis among them, were yelling and pointing at the place where she had gone in. The sun was off the cove now, the water there darkly shadowed. They would not be able to see the bottom.

Demetria pulled the knitting bag round to lie across her back and dived again. The next time she came up she was afraid she might be seen, but she was a good way out now. She began to swim, fast, hard, to where her log would be coming to meet her. The going was tougher than she had expected. Waves broke over her head and Tycho was strong, she was swimming against it, but there was nowhere to go except onwards until she met the log or until she grew so tired that she could only float, and then let Tycho take her down.

When she reached the log it was bigger than she had ever imagined, but it had been a long time in the sea and it was riding low in the water at the wider end. It did not roll when she struggled on board. She was still in sight of land, she must keep a low profile. Lying flat, Demetria tugged the lifeline from the bag and pinned it to a crack in the bark with one of the steel knitting needles. Then she dived again, under the log, and brought the line with her; once more and the log was securely girdled. She had a handle to grasp and, clinging to it, rolled back in the water, letting the whale tow her. Only then did she think, How did I know what to do?

Nothing had been planned, she had never made preparations because she had never really believed that she would do this, yet somehow, without

211

knowing it, she had been getting ready, so that when she went down to the cove and saw the log ploughing through the waves alone, she had known that it was coming for her.

But almost she had not made it in time. The log was gathering speed now as it entered the strait. No one was in pursuit. Either they thought she had drowned and were searching the cove, or they had given up, supposing that Tycho had taken her. She did not care either way.

It would not be safe to climb back aboard until she was clear of the Low Island. The log was very close to its shore, only a few hundred metres out, and she wondered if the prisoners ever tried to trap logs. She stayed close to the side of her whale, only eyes and nose above the water, and saw why it was called the Low Island. There were no hills, no cliffs, only banks of shingle along the shoreline. And now she could see clearly the buildings – rows of huts with metal roofs like the barracks on the mole, the watch towers, the wire, the pylons that carried the floodlights.

She did not see people. She could only wonder, Are you there?

When all that was far behind her she hauled herself out of the water. The sun was almost down now. Soon the lighthouse would come on. She took off the apron that she need never wear again, tied it to the line and sat back to see what she had caught and tamed. The log must be twenty metres long, and at her end the part out of the water was nearly two metres wide. In the knitting bag she had the remains of her dinner: food in the oilskin pouch and a bottle of cold tea. When that was gone it would be easy to scoop up handfuls of sea when she needed to drink. Sea-water tasted foul, like sucking an iron bar, but it was drinkable, even if it made your tongue shrivel, as she had heard it did. Her clothes were drying on her, stiff and tight, but she could soon work them loose again. She fastened herself to the free end of the line, but not too tightly. If the log should turn over she would not be trapped underneath. She knew what being trapped underwater felt like.

It was growing dark. Over her left shoulder lights were springing up on the prison island; over her right the lighthouse swept the strait. When she saw that she turned round and for the first time in her life saw the High Island, her home, rising in a rugged cone from its vertical cliffs to the apex of the peak that was still growing golden with sunset. Little lights pricked its lower slopes but already they were fainter than the stars. It was going, it was going. She would watch until the peak itself had gone and then turn her face away. Meanwhile there was something to be done. She began to untie the remains of her plait.

The long heavy rope of it had gone, left behind on the kitchen table, and the nine thick strands had become loose on their own. All that remained were the twenty-seven braids that had dragged her

213

eyebrows up, stretched her mouth, flattened her nose. She walked her fingers over her face, exploring. Her mouth was still wide, her nose just as flat, perhaps they always would be, but as each braid came undone she seemed to feel another weight drop away.

At last they were all free. She had thought that the wind would lift her unbound hair so that it fluttered about her head, but all it did was stir the little loose ends around her neck and forehead. The rest needed time to dry and unfold. She wished that she could comb it out but she had no comb. She had never needed one.

And she had never seen a mirror, depending entirely on what Stephane had told her she looked like, until Ianto Morgan had given her a different picture. But she could picture herself now, aboard her whale, heading fearless and windswept into the unknown.

Would Ianto Morgan have come back for her? She had made his escape for him, in a way; perhaps one day she would come back for him.

The moon came up, the little tumbling rock. That was what had started it all. *Call that a moon?* If he had not said that she would never have known that there was any other kind of moon, and other kinds of worlds, any other way of living.

She was trembling now, not from cold, not from fear or even excitement, but from something that had not caught up with her yet. If Bevis and Brodie had

214

not seen her going down to the cove, had not converged on her as she stood barefoot on the ledge, would she have dared to step into the sea and swim out to her whale, or would she have sat there, desperate, wretched, too scared, too sensible, to do the mad thing that she had done, setting herself adrift on a log that might circle the oceans of Demeter forever?

Tomorrow, by daylight, she would know what she had done. For now she would keep watch as she had promised herself. The island was swallowed in darkness; in spite of its height the peak was lost among the stars. But the lighthouse shone on, its swingeing beam scarcely more than a flicker on the horizon and then it too was gone. She turned away and stood upright, feet apart, braced on the log, and felt it surge beneath her, riding Tycho into the night. Overhead, the little tumbling rock continued its own brave, lonely voyage among the stars.

From Voyager, *the sequel to* Riding Tycho

The instructions about drifting logs were clear and simple. The smaller ones could be ignored, but anything over four metres must be taken in tow and brought to land. Often half-submerged and yawing unpredictably, they were a hazard to small craft, and the log sighted by the crew of the *Laurentia Bay* was a giant, twenty metres at least, almost as long as the vessel itself. It was passing them on the starboard beam and as the helmsman put her about they had time to assemble the chains and grappling hooks, but as the *Laurentia Bay* bore down on her quarry one of the seamen called out that there was something odd about this one.

Halfway along its length was a thing – he could not come up with a better word – some kind of a plant perhaps or a seaweed that had taken root. As they gathered to look the boat drew closer and they could see that it was a bushy tangle of white threads, some matted, some loose and blowing in the sea wind; springy, spiralling, apparently growing out of the trunk which still had long scabs of bark adhering to it. Then there was another shout, startled and wary. Whatever the strange growth was, there seemed to be a living creature under it.

When the *Laurentia Bay* came alongside they could

see it clearly. It looked almost human; they could make out impossibly thin limbs, bony hands and feet, all burned dark brown, almost black, by long exposure to the sun. As they leaned over for a closer look they saw that the growth of white fibres, under which it hid or sheltered, was its hair.

They had sailed the tideless oceans of Demeter all their lives, and seen marvellous sights. Being men with little learning and mightily superstitious, they had made the sights more marvellous in the telling. This was something they had told of but never seen.

One of them said, 'Mermaid?'

'It's got legs.'

'It may have a tail as well.'

'Where's its head?'

'Shut your gibbering faces and get the hooks ready.' The bosun was as curious as any of them. He did not believe it was a mermaid but he did not think it looked fully human, either; such dark skin, such white hair. Still, it was clear to him exactly what it was. 'Two of you get down on that log now!'

They were reluctant to go. The thing had started to stir. At the bosun's shout it opened its eyes, mere slits in the taut skin of its face that looked more like tanned leather than anything living, and gazed up at them. The head did not move but the eyes fixed themselves on the prow which had just come level with it.

Whatever it saw frightened it terribly, and without getting up it began to scrabble with its hind claws at the trunk where it was sprawled. The forepaws, with their blunted nails, paddled uselessly as if it were trying to swim. It was a weak and feeble monster but it started to creep forward and the great horrible quivering mass of its hair crept with it.

'Get it, catch it,' someone cried. 'Quick, before it dives in.'

The happy thought of what they could do with a monster got them moving. The landsmen's law forbade exhibiting monsters unless they were dead, in which case collectors had been known to pay. But there were people on shore who would be interested in a live one, and this monster looked as if it would be easy to catch. For all its frantic pawing it had moved barely a metre and now they could see that it was tethered to the log by a length of orange twine.

Two of the crew went over the side, boarded the log and converged upon the creature. It struggled slightly and croaked, but put up no real resistance, and it was very light to handle although neither of them much wanted to touch it. There was something unwholesome about that hair. When the seaman severed the orange cord and threw the creature over his shoulder the hair, instead of hanging down, remained in a rigid sphere like a giant seed head.

To be continued . . .